J.T. EDSON'S
FLOATING OUTFIT

The toughest bunch of Rebels that ever lost a war, they fought for the South, and then for Texas, as the legendary Floating Outfit of "Ole Devil" Hardin's O.D. Connected ranch.

MARK COUNTER was the best-dressed man in the West: always dressed fit-to-kill. **BELLE BOYD** was as deadly as she was beautiful, with a "Manhattan" model Colt tucked under her long skirts. **THE YSABEL KID** was Comanche fast and Texas tough. And the most famous of them all was **DUSTY FOG**, the ex-cavalryman known as the Rio Hondo Gun Wizard.

J. T. Edson has captured all the excitement and adventure of the raw frontier in this magnificent Western series. Turn the page for a list of Floating Outfit titles.

J. T. EDSON'S
FLOATING OUTFIT
WESTERN ADVENTURES

J. T. EDSON'S
CIVIL WAR SERIES

OTHER BOOKS BY J. T. EDSON

J.T. Edson

THE RUSHERS

CHARTER BOOKS, NEW YORK

This book was originally published
in Great Britain by Brown Watson, Limited

This Charter book contains the complete
text of the original edition.
It has been completely reset in a typeface
designed for easy reading and was printed
from new film.

THE RUSHERS

A Charter Book/published by arrangement with
Transworld Publishers, Ltd.

PRINTING HISTORY
Brown Watson edition published 1964
Corgi edition published 1969
Berkley edition / September 1982
Charter edition / November 1989

ISBN: 1-55773-301-5

Charter Books are published by The Berkley Publishing Group,
200 Madison Avenue, New York, N.Y. 10016.
The name "CHARTER" and the "C" logo are
trademarks belonging to Charter Communications, Inc.

PRINTED IN THE UNITED STATES OF AMERICA

10 9 8 7 6 5 4 3 2 1

For Pat and Dave Symons

CHAPTER ONE

Dandy Van Druten's End

Captain van Druten's career came to an end as a result of his own stupidity. Transferred to the 15th Cavalry, he received orders to take command of a battalion based at Fort Tucker. Instead of travelling with a replacement sergeant-major and a party of recruits, he took the civilian scout, left word where he would meet the detachment, and set off on a hunting trip. On his way to the rendezvous, fate, in the shape of four young Sioux bucks, took a hand. The small captain—family influence gained him his commission and held him in it— died as he took off his hat to wipe his forehead, a bullet shattering his skull. An instant later the scout dropped at his side.

While stripping their victims prior to mutilating the bodies, one of the braves glanced up, saw something and died as he opened his mouth to give warning. Three rifle-armed white men sat horses on the slope above them, but before the remaining bucks could make a move, two more died.

The last brave went for his horse in racing strides, bounding up. On the rim the black-dressed rider on the huge white stallion followed the Sioux with his rifle, taking careful sight. His finger squeezed the trigger as the brave bounded up to his horse. Even though he landed on the horse the Sioux had taken lead, his lifeless

1

body slid off the other side and the horse sprang forward.

Weapons held ready for use, the three men rode down the slope. While young, each one bore a legendary name; although they would be better known on a more southerly range than the Dakota Territory.

At the right, sitting his huge blood-bay stallion with the relaxed grace of a light rider despite his giant size, rode Mark Counter. Six foot three inches tall, with wide shoulders and a slender waist, with the classic features of a Greek god and the muscular development of a Hercules. His costly, low-crowned, wide-brimmed Texas-style J.B. Stetson hat sat back on his curly golden-blond hair and shielded the handsome face from the sun. His clothes were costly and he wore them well, with the air of a dandy. Yet the brown leather buscadero gunbelt and the matched ivory-handled Colt Cavalry Peacemakers in the holsters were both practical and showed the signs of belonging to a fast man with a gun. In his powerful right hand he held one of the new center-fire .44.40 Winchester rifles, the gun soon to be known as the model of 1873 and replacing the odd brass-framed model of 1866 such as the rider at the left carried.

Sitting his white stallion with a relaxed, almost Indian-like grace, the Ysabel Kid looked down at the bodies with little or no emotion. Six foot of slim, wiry and deadly manhood the Kid nevertheless contrived to look as young and innocent as a choirboy in church. His hair was black as the wing of a deep-south crow, his face tanned, young looking and almost babyishly handsome. Yet the eyes were neither young nor innocent. They were hard, cold, menacing, red-hazel in color and with a touch of hell in them. The Kid wore all black, from hat, through bandana, shirt, levis, down to boots. Even his gunbelt had been made of black leather and only the ivory hilt of the James Black bowie knife at his left and the walnut grips of the old Second Model Dragoon Colt butt forward at his right relieved the blackness. He cradled the old "yellow boy" Winchester '66 rifle across his arm, looking as wild, alien and cruel as the Sioux before they fell.

Riding in the center of the trio Dusty Fog alone did not appear to be the kind of man who made a name for himself. In height he stood at most five foot six and, when among his taller friends, people were apt to discount the breadth of shoulders which told of a muscle packed and powerful body. He wore just as costly clothes as either of his friends, yet did not have the flair for setting them off to their full advantage. Just as Mark Counter could look elegantly attired in old rags, Dusty was able to wear the best clothes money could buy and make them look like nothing. His hair had a dusty blond color, the face was handsome, strong yet not in Mark's eye-catching manner. Around his waist the gunbelt, with the matched brace of bone-handled Colt Civilian Peacemakers, butt forwards for a cross draw, in the holsters, did not look dangerous. For so insignificant appearing a young man the huge paint stallion looked out of place. One so ordinary looking should never own or ride so fine an animal as the paint. Yet own and ride it he did and there were few others who could even claim to have tried and failed to ride Dusty Fog's big paint. He sat relaxed in the saddle, holding a Winchester '73 carbine, preferring the shorter, twenty-inch barrel and the twelve- instead of sixteen-round magazine capacity for its better handling qualities in saddle use.

Strange as it may seem, of the three men the small insignificant Texan called Dusty Fog, had made a name which ranked higher than the other two, more eye-catching though they might be.

First in the Civil War, as a Confederate cavalry captain at seventeen, Dusty Fog rose to fame. His name ranked with Turner Ashby and John Singleton Mosby as a raider in the military sense of the word. He led a troop of fast-riding, hard-hitting Texans and built a name for courage, ability, gallantry and chivalry even among his Union Army enemies. After the War men spoke of Dusty as tophand cowboy, segundo of Ole Devil Hardin's mighty OD Connected cattle outfit, leader of the elite of a tough and capable crew. Ole Devil's floating outfit. He built a name as a trail boss, running the cattle herds north to the Kansas shipping pens. Men spoke of him also as a town taming lawman who brought peace and tamed Quiet Town after lesser men died trying.

Mostly they spoke of Dusty Fog's speed on the draw, his accuracy once the guns were clear. His name stood high on the list of the knights of the tied-down holster. In all he did he stood head and shoulders above his fellows despite his lack of inches.

Mark Counter also carried a well-known name. The Texan cowhands claimed Mark knew his trade better than Dusty Fog even. His dress style set the fashion for the rangeland dandies from East Texas to the New Mexico line. His strength was a legend, his prowess in a rough-house brawl spoken of with bated breath by all who witnessed it. Yet few could say just how good or fast he was with his matched Colts. Those who did know claimed him to be fast, very fast, and accurate too. Yet there were few who knew for Mark Counter dwelled in the shadow of the Rio Hondo gun-wizard, Dusty Fog, and his true prowess remained hidden in the shade.

The final member of the trio had a name. Loncey Dalton Ysabel, the Ysabel Kid, *el Cabrito* the border Mexicans whispered when they spoke of him among themselves. Friend of many, terror of those who were not his friends, down on the Rio Grande that was how the Ysabel Kid had been known. Those days, when he ran contraband across the river with his father, had long gone by. Now he rode with Dusty and Mark in the floating outfit and was scout in time of war. His father gave him a sturdy but truculent spirit, a sighting eye like an eagle or a mountain man of old. From the blood of Chief Long Walker, old man chief of the dreaded Dog Soldier lodge, came the Kid's ability to ride anything with hair, to follow a trail where a buck Apache might falter, to know and understand Indians and read the ways of nature. From the French-Creole came a love of cold steel as a weapon which made him retain that wicked bowie knife at his side and use it as his pet weapon for close-range war. These qualities were all in the one package and made an explosive bundle which might have gone off the wrong way but for joining Dusty Fog. Now the Kid had a name for being a good friend to those he gave his loyalty and friendship, but a real bad enemy to any who crossed him.

On hearing of thousands of gold-hungry people gathering in the Dakotas, Dusty knew there would be a market for beef. So he gathered a herd and brought it north. Apart from his two friends, all the rest of the trail crew stayed on to try to make a fortune. Dusty, Mark, and the Kid ignored the rumors of "gold at the grass roots," remembering that the Black Hills were regarded as sacred land by the Indians and had been given in solemn treaty to the Sioux. The three friends had started their journey home when they came upon the sight of the Sioux, although arriving too late to save van Druten or the scout.

Dropping from his saddle, the Kid examined the bodies. "They're all cashed, Dusty," he said.

Working swiftly, the Texans buried van Druten and the scout under a pile of rocks, dragged the Sioux away and hid as much of the sign of sudden death as they could. Taking van Druten's belongings and horse to hand over to the first army post they found, the three young men continued their interrupted journey.

The day was drawing to a close when the Texans brought their horses to a halt and listened to the distant crackle of gunfire. Advancing cautiously, they topped a rim and saw the cause of the shooting. Using van

Druten's field glasses, Dusty studied the situation. He did not like what he saw.

About half a mile away, near a spring, six army wagons formed an oblong of defense for the men within. The soldiers appeared to be in a good position, their horses picketed in lines within the oblong, boxes making a barricade under and between the wagons. Surrounding the oblong, making a determined attack, the Sioux appeared to be in strength, over two hundred of them, mostly armed with bows or lances, but with enough firearms of various kinds to make things real interesting for all concerned.

Studying the soldiers, Dusty knew them to be unblooded recruits in their first fight. Even as he watched, Dusty saw the sergeant-major commanding the party crumple and fall. Instantly near-panic and uncertainty ran through the camp. Fortunately the Sioux were withdrawing to make fresh medicine or the circle would have been broken. One more rush and the leaderless soldiers would be finished.

The Sioux had all gathered, or most, for they left a few men on the other flanks, to one side. They sat their horses, watching the old medicine-man as he raised his arms to the sky, gripping the war lance between them as he called down the air of their great war god. He would make his medicine, give courage and strength to the brave-heart warriors so that they would sweep down and overwhelm the soldier-coats and wagons.

"We've not got long afore the medicine's made," drawled the Kid. "Then, less I never seen a bad Injun, it'll be like a Christmas turkey shoot with those blue belly boys for the turkeys."

"We've got to go shake those boys together, Dusty," Mark stated after studying the scene through the field glasses.

"Be a tolerable pile of dead Yankee scalps on the Sioux lodge poles if we don't," was the Kid's summing up of the situation. "Happen we run down that dry wash there and don't meet any Sioux in it, we can get to within a hundred yards or so of the wagons. Go across faster'n fast, hit that small bunch of braves there and we might get through afore the main bunch know what's hit them—unless the soldier boys inside spook and shoot us first.''

Dusty agreed with his friends and already formed his plan, but also saw its difficulties. The soldiers were not veterans who could recognize a leader no matter how he dressed. To the recruits, a leader wore either stripes on his sleeves or bars on his shoulders. If Dusty were to save the soldiers, he must be able to take command of them from the moment he landed in their midst. Given time, he could win the men over, but time was something he did not have.

Despite the difficulty of the decision, Dusty only hesitated for a moment. It did not come easily, for Dusty remembered the aftermath of the War Between the States, but he went ahead with his plan. Swiftly he stripped off his hat, boots and levis, replacing them with the dead captain's clothing. The uniform fitted him well; it was strange how two men so different in character should be so physically alike.

Setting his borrowed campaign hat at the old jaunty angle, Dusty looked to where Mark was packing his cowhand clothing into his bedroll. Somehow Dusty had changed, looked less inconspicuous and more of his real self as he strapped on his gunbelt. Wanting a horse he could trust under hm, he vaulted into the paint's saddle.

"Let's go," he said.

They rode along the drywash, finding no Sioux in it. However, a small bunch of braves sat horses between the Texans and the wagon circle.

"You pair all set?" asked Dusty in a whisper.

"Tomorrow'd be a better day, or next fall," replied the Kid. "Only they just won't haul off and wait that long for us."

"Straight down and through that bunch, Dusty?" asked Mark, drawing his right-hand Colt.

"Straight down and through," agreed Dusty. "Whooping like a drunk Kiowa on his way to a wedding."

"Best ride instead of whittle-whanging about it," drawled the Kid. "Afore some of those Sioux see us here and take offence at us for peeking. They've near on said their prayers over the back and are getting ready to go."

Drawing his left-hand Colt, Dusty took out van Druten's sabre with his right hand, finding its edge sharp enough for what he needed.

The Kid watched the Sioux, although he could not hear the words he read the signs and the meaning of the prayer. His eyes had a hellish gleam in them and his face twisted into the grin of a Comanche Dog Soldier about to make a joke such as slitting an enemy's throat from ear to ear.

"That old medicine-man there, Dusty," he said. "He's just telling the great Manitou they've done killed the leader of the soldiers and that victory'll be all their'n right soon. Which same you arriving there full of fancy buttons, shoulder bars and all's sure going to make his medicine look awful watered down."

"If we get through," grinned Mark.

"You're tolerable safe, *amigo*," replied the Kid. "Only the good go young, which same you're here for ever and I'm past where I should have gone."

Dusty smiled, then his face went grim once more. His friends were mounted ready, the Kid holding his rifle, fully loaded once more and all set to make some good Indians. Mark held his right-hand Colt and unfastened the dead officer's horse, for he did not wish to be hampered.

"You go or stay, hoss," he said quietly. "But I'm sure not trying to haul you after me."

"Eeeeyah!"

The rebel war-yell shattered the air, ringing echoes back against the walls of the dry wash. Dusty gave it, then set his spurs to the flanks of the huge paint. Like a raging Texas twister the three horses hurled from the mouth of the dry wash. They went towards the oblong of wagons like the devil after a yearling. The cavalry horse followed, racing by their side. Straight at the startled bunch of Sioux tore the three fast riding men, two civilians and the other, every inch, a Union army captain.

CHAPTER TWO

Captain Fog Assumes Command

Watching the medicine-making ceremony at the other side of the camp, the dozen or so Sioux between the Texans and the wagons realized their danger a full fifteen seconds too late. They heard the drumming of the hooves and the wild yells and turned to face three hard-riding white men each handling a lead-spitting weapon with deadly accuracy. Taken by surprise, with three of their number down in the first seconds of the rush, the braves scattered and the Texans passed through them unscathed. Cavalry-trained, van Druten's horse ran at Dusty's side and followed the small Texan through the gap into the wagon circle. Even as the three Texans joined the soldiers, a hideous roar rose from the remainder of the Sioux and another attack began.

"Here they come!" whooped the Kid, jerking a box of bullets from his saddle-pouch and sprinting after Dusty.

Faced by the awe-inspiring charge, the recruits showed signs of panic. Even the Ysabel Kid, who usually claimed that only Comanche and Apache were real *bad* Indians, conceded that the attacking Hunkpapa Sioux looked tolerable mean *hombres* and right likely to make things lively in a fight.

Leaping from his saddle, Dusty glared at a young corporal who seemed as panic-stricken as the rest of the men.

10

"Corporal!" Dusty roared, just as the young non-com prepared to bolt for safety. "What the hell are you doing?"

His voice stiffened the men. It might hold a Texas drawl but through it ran the cold hardness of a tough officer who spoke and expected immediate obedience, the sort of man who was obeyed instantly—or else, somebody wished he had been. The corporal threw a scared look over his shoulder, took in Dusty's uniform and did not doubt for a minute that their new commanding officer, Captain Marcus van Druten, stood behind him.

"We was try——"

"Then don't!" barked Dusty. "Are your men loaded?"

The corporal clearly did not know but Dusty knew he would have no time to check. He could only hope that the sergeant-major gave the order to reload before taking lead.

"Take aim!" he ordered and the rifles lined. "Line carefully and make every shot count. Fire!"

The resulting volley was ragged and Dusty roared out an order which sent hands to working the trap-door breeches of the Springfield carbines, then shoving home another round as the empty cases flew out. Three Sioux had gone down before the volley but from either end of the line came the whip-like cracking of Mark and the Kid's rifles. Neither of them needed any telling what they must do and acted fast. The rapid fire cut among the Indians, emptying the backs of racing ponies or tumbling the animals.

A scared young recruit twisted around towards Dusty and the small Texan hurled forward. This was no time for gentle words or actions. One hint of weakness would allow the men time to let their fear override the discipline drove into them since joining the army. Dusty sent the sabre point into the ground, then his right hand came around, the back of it driving into the soldier's face and spinning him around into the wagon.

"The next man who looks away from the Sioux will be shot!" Dusty warned. "Fire at random. Keep firing!"

Under the hail of fire the Sioux attack broke, splitting and carrying on around the oblong of wagons. Dusty watched. The flanks, not being faced with the solid awe-inspiring rush, handled themselves well, keeping up a fire which held the Sioux back. Now and then a brave or small group, would try a rush at the wagons. They came fast and were the worst danger of all. Let them get inside the circle and the rest would take heart, pressing home their attack so superior weight of numbers must crush down the soldiers.

Dusty seemed to be everywhere at once, racing from point to point, always when needed, stiffening and directing the defense. He bore a charmed life for he had become the prime target of the Sioux. Their medicine had been made on the assumption that the soldier-coats were leaderless. Now a new leader had come in and led the defense.

In the hectic moments following the charge, Dusty made a complete circle of the wagon area. He did not have time to speak with the sergeant-major in passing, for the man lay by a wagon, his tunic ripped open and his shoulder bandaged. The medical orderly looked up at Dusty, opened his mouth to speak, thought better of it and darted to where a soldier lay on the ground with an arrow buried flight deep in his chest.

On reaching the side where the first rush came Dusty saw it could safely be left to Mark and the Kid. They knew how to control men and their repeating rifles gave the eight soldiers heart to fight.

Then it was over. The Sioux pulled back in disorder, leaving a number of their braves dead on the ground. The Kid watched them draw back until they lined the slopes surrounding the wagons. He walked towards Mark, thumbing bullets through the loading slot of his Winchester.

"That'll hold them for a spell, likely until nightfall and they don't make war in the dark. At most they won't more than once today."

"Which same could be enough," Mark replied. "Ole Dusty sure pulled these blue bellies together, didn't he?"

"He sure did," grinned the Kid. "Just look at them bunch who took the main rush. They're all puffed up with themselves like they'd whupped the whole Sioux nation."

The change in the men showed plain. No longer did they look scared. Instead all were grinning broadly, even though the faces might be a greyish tinge under the newly gained tan. They'd stood up to an attack, beat it off and could claim to be fighting men at last.

Dusty did not get a chance to speak with his two friends as he walked around the defenses once more. He wanted to speak with the sergeant-major, get the uniform off and return to wearing his own clothes. A bullet fired at long range hissed by his head but he ignored it. Then Dusty saw something which roused his anger. One of the soldiers had rested his rifle against the wheel of a wagon and was looking around him without regard to the watching Sioux.

"Do I look like an Indian!" Dusty roared, almost leaping forward.

The soldier found himself confronted by an angry officer, a man with hard, cold and savage eyes. He stiffened into a brace, his mouth suddenly felt dry and he knew better than try any flip answers with this officer who came so dramatically to their rescue.

"No—no—no, cap'n sir," he gasped.

"Then why in hell's name are you looking at me?" demanded Dusty, his voice throbbing with anger. "Keep your full attention on the Sioux or I'll have you lashed to an outside wagon wheel where you can see them properly!"

From the tone of Dusty's voice the young soldier did

not for a moment doubt the threat would be carried out, nor did any of the others who heard. Not one of them took their eyes from the surrounding line of braves, but one called:

"They're shooting at us, cap'n, sir."

"That's all right. They're not on our side so they're allowed to."

As a joke it wouldn't have made Eddie Foy fear for his act but it served to bring a chuckle from the men. Dusty knew better than to keep riding them and now that they were all attending to duty could relax slightly.

Dusty walked to where the wounded sergeant-major lay. The man was tall, wide shouldered and burly, clearly an old soldier, a man who had seen plenty of action in his time. The bullet had grazed his shoulder badly, spun him into the side of a wagon and his head struck as he went down, knocking him unconscious. He had regained consciousness now and tried to stiffen into a brace as Dusty dropped to his knees by the wounded man's side.

"Hogan, sir," said the non-com. "Sergeant-major. We've been three days at the rendezvous, sir, waiting for you."

In the voice Dusty detected a faint hint of disapproval. His eyes narrowed a trifle for he was not a man to allow his rank to be flouted. Then he realized the sergeant-major took him to be the dead officer. Dusty's eyes could detect nothing in Hogan's face, certainly not a thing to indicate Hogan might be an officer-hater who hid behind the limits of the *Manual of Field Regulations* to deride and belittle his superiors. Hogan struck Dusty as being a good man with a legitimate grievance against the dead captain.

"I got your orders at Fort Bannard, sir," Hogan went on. "You'd left before I could see you and taken the only scout available. The regiment pulled out the day we left, sir, they've been ordered to the south and needed all their scouts. I came by map and formed a circle to wait for you."

"Mister," drawled Dusty quietly, so that none but Hogan might hear his words. "The officer you expected won't be coming. He's back there a piece with no top to his head. Him and the scout both are dead."

For a moment Hogan did not reply. He looked as if he could not believe the evidence of his ears. His eyes went to the uniform, the way it fitted Dusty and the general look of the small Texan.

"But you—I saw the way you came in and took over."

"Somebody had to, friend. You were down and those green recruits likely to spook on the next attack. I knew they wouldn't take orders from a civilian, not fast enough to do any good. The Sioux had stripped your captain and we brought his clothes along with us, in case we run across soldiers, or found a fort to leave them with. Knew the army'd want to know what happened to him and figured his kin'd like to have his belongings. So when I saw how things stood I put the uniform on and got in here."

Hogan still stared at Dusty. In twenty-eight years of army service he'd learned to recognize the real thing when it came before him. No matter what this small Texan said nothing would convince Hogan that he did not look at a real tough, all-army, officer. The way the men shook into shape at the Texan's command gave full proof of that.

"You've got to carry on doing it c—mister," Hogan said, just biting off the formal "captain, sir" as he spoke. "I'm not steady enough to hold them together and the Sioux'll come back again. You'll do it, won't you?"

"There's no other way," Dusty replied. "What's the strength of the command?"

"Thirty recruits for Fort Tucker, sir, one medical

orderly, six wagons with supplies, two men in each wagon. We'd lost two men before I fell, sir."

Strangely Hogan did not feel anything unusual about saying "sir" to Dusty. He could not shake off the feeling that he addressed an officer, a very efficient officer of at least captain's rank.

"Rest easy," Dusty drawled. "I'll take over."

He came to his feet and looked around. The horses, picketed on lines across the open, seemed safe enough. He wanted to see the men, have them before him and form an impression of their state to carry on the fight.

"Fall in here!" he barked. "Lon, Mark, watch the Sioux."

"Yo!" came Mark's cavalry reply.

"They've pulled back to make more medicine," called the Kid.

This was always the Sioux way of fighting. Once an attack failed the braves gathered and made fresh medicine, trying to decide why the old batch failed them and whether it would be advisable to make another attack. They never realized that by so doing they gave their enemy a chance to reorganize and prepare for further defense.

The order brought men running to form up before Dusty in double file, standing at attention and giving Dusty a chance to look them over in the manner of a new officer studying his men for the first time. With the men standing in line, backs to the wagons, the Sioux might have taken a chance at easy coups but they were at their medicine and the Kid stood with his rifle ready to prevent any easy coups being made.

With cold eyes Dusty studied the men before him, walking along the front rank until he came to halt before the corporal.

"I've seen worse but I'm damned if I know where," Dusty said coldly. "Account for your ammunition, corporal."

The corporal gulped nervously. "I—I don't know for sure."

Out shot Dusty's right hand, gripping the stripes and ripping them from the corporal's sleeve. His eyes never left the startled soldier's face, daring him to as much as breathe in protest. The corporal kept rigid at his brace, lips tight together, for one thing a man learned early in the army was to keep his mouth shut at such a moment.

"Account for your ammunition," Dusty said to the private soldier next to the now stripeless corporal.

"Ten rounds for my carbine and twelve combustible cartridges for my revolver, plus the six loads in the Colt."

"Take rank as corporal," said Dusty. "Move out here, man. Check every man's supply of ammunition, then resupply those who need it."

"Yo!" snapped the soldier and moved from the line.

"Divide the troop equally for defense of the four sides," Dusty went on. "Four men to attend to the horses."

Recruit or not the young soldier went into action fast. From the way he took command he would go far in the army. Dusty stood back and watched his orders obeyed, then made arrangements for the men to be fed. He sent sentries to each side allowing Mark and the Kid to attend to their three horses, for not one of the big stallions would take kindly to strangers handling them and the Kid's big white could be very dangerous to any who tried.

Finally, when all in the camp satisfied him, Dusty returned to the big sergeant-major who had propped himself up against the wagon wheel, the better to see how things went and to lend Dusty moral and verbal support if needed. A grin split Hogan's face as Dusty came to his side.

"You're not trying to tell a man twenty-eight years in the army that you've never before held officer's rank?"

he asked, as Dusty bent to check the bandage. "Sure and I'd never believe that."

"Wouldn't huh?"

"I wouldn't. There's army in everything you do and say. Who are you?"

"I rode in the Texas Light Cavalry in the War," Dusty replied.

Hogan nodded. "A good fighting outfit, even if they were volunteers. Sure they handled them——"The words died away and he stared at Dusty. "The Saints preserve us. You're him."

"Who?"

"Captain Dusty Fog. Sure and I should have seen it from the first. There's devil of a few men who could or wouldn've done what you did."

Dusty felt a glow of pleasure and some pride as he saw the admiring look in the eyes of the hard-bitten sergeant-major. They rode on opposite sides in the war yet Hogan could still retain a true soldier's admiration for a brave and gallant enemy.

"And Dandy van Druten's dead, is he," Hogan went on. "May the devil ride on his pillow. I looked to have hell under him at Fort Tucker, it'll be a restive command I've got for all of that, no commanding officer and under three shavetail lieutenants for nearly a month. Sure and it'll be a firm hand that's needed to quieten down the buckos at the Fort."

Mark and the Kid came towards the two men and were introduced to Hogan. The Kid wasted no time in small talk but pointed to the slope where most of the Sioux had gathered once more.

"Taking a tolerable time to make their medicine," he said. "Like I figured out there," he waved a hand to where they'd been watching the fight from the rim, "the old medicine-man made his play on their downing you, friend. Only Dusty coming busting in like that spoiled it for them. Now he's calling down on the war gods and making his mind up whether to hit us again afore dark,

leave it until dawn for a big rush, or call off the fight
and ride out.''

''Which'll it be?'' asked Dusty.

''I don't know, one or the other of them for sure. I
allow he's got but one more losing attack afore they
claim his medicine's gone real sour and want to pull out
of it.''

Suddenly the man on sentry at the side through which
Dusty and the other two made their appearance, let out
a yell, pointing. Dusty and his two friends went racing
forward as, from the same dry wash they used, a rider
burst into sight. He came fast, riding with death as a
spur, for he came alone and towards some twenty
Sioux.

''Take your posts!'' roared the young soldier Dusty
illegally promoted to corporal. ''Move it, shake the
bull-droppings from your socks!''

Dusty reached the side of the wagon, knocking the
sentry's rifle into the air before he could fire. The rider
came straight at the wagons, clear of the Sioux but they
had come swarming towards him and at a charge. For
all that he rode a big Sioux paint and dressed in
buckskins the newcomer was no Indian. His face had a
tan, but the long hair which showed from under his hat
was red, not Indian black. The Henry rifle in his hands
crashed fast as he rode, he tumbled a brave over. Then
he swung the Henry to fire from waist high into the face
of a second Sioux just as the brave came charging in to
skewer him on the end of a lance.

''Hold your fire!'' Dusty roared to the men who came
rushing up.

At such a time volley firing would not be the answer,
for the Sioux closed in around and behind the fast riding
man. A skilled and careful aim was needed at this moment, not a mass of shots directed towards the enemy.

''Pour it on, Lon, Mark!'' he ordered.

Two rifles began to crack, rifles handled by men who
could call their shots. Mark sighted and shot at a brave

who drew back a bow ready to send a buffalo arrow between the newcomer's shoulder blades. The brave tilted
backwards, his arrow flying into the air. At the same instant the Kid chopped a rifle-armed brave from his
horse by sending a bullet within inches of the fast-riding
white man.

The rider made the circle, his horse sailing over the
barricade and coming to a rump-scraping halt. Dusty
ordered off a volley, his voice acting as a spur, raking
home and causing every trigger-finger to squeeze. The
shots ripped out, two more braves and a horse fell, then
the rest retreated to a safe distance.

Dropping from his horse the man came towards
Dusty. He stood an inch or so over six foot, with wide
shoulders slanting down to a lean waist. From the battered campaign hat he wore, his buckskins and the army
belt around his waist, a Remington Army revolver in the
holster and a bowie knife at the other side, Dusty took
the man to be a civilian scout.

"Howdy, captain," the man said, shifting his Henry
to his left hand, holding the right out. "Name's Jim
Halter, chief scout out to Fort Tucker. Mr. Gilbert, him
being senior officer there, sent me to look for you."

Watching the man's tanned, handsome face Dusty
could read no hint of trickery in it. The small Texan had
not overlooked the possibility of this being a renegade
white man, a friend of the Sioux, trying to trick the
soldiers into a fool move which would lay them wide
open for an attack.

Halter went to his horse and pulled an envelope from
the saddle-pouch, then returned to hand it to Dusty. His
eyes went to the Sioux on the slopes, flickered to the setting sun and he grunted.

"That'll be all for today, unless they make another
attack real soon. I reckon seeing your men standing to
by the wagons, scared them off."

"Sure," agreed the Ysabel Kid. "I thought they was

all set to make a rush when you shot out and the young
corporal there got the others into place. It sure scared
that old medicine-man up there. He called off the attack
right on the spot.''

The scout's eyes went to the Kid, looking beyond the
innocent face and not needing to ask how so young a
man knew about Indians, not even needing to ask how a
Texas cowhand came to know what Sioux thought. Jim
Halter was a quarter Blackfoot and knew another part-
Indian when he saw one.

''You'd best come down this way,'' Dusty drawled.

Halter came with Dusty and the Kid attended to the
scout's horse. The scout had a puzzled glint in his eyes
which did not clear up when he saw the wounded
sergeant-major. He watched Dusty give orders for the
men to stand down, then rubbed his jaw as if thinking
hard.

''This's Sergeant-Major Hogan,'' Dusty said.

''And you?'' asked Halter. ''I came across a riderless
hoss, knew it belonged to Billy Cragg, a scout from Fort
Bannard, so I backtracked it. Found Billy and another
man dead and buried under a pile of rocks, scouted and
found four dead Sioux. Then picked up the trail of four
hosses, one without a rider, brought me here. Only the
man with Cragg, he'd got him an army shirt on, officer's white shirt.''

''That was the late and unlamented Captain van
Druten,'' growled Hogan grimly. ''This here's Captain
Fog.''

For a moment Halter did not reply, then slowly he
nodded his head. ''Captain Dusty Fog?''

''The same,'' repied Hogan.

''Never knowed you were in the U.S. cavalry, Cap'n
Fog.''

''I'm not,'' Dusty answered quietly, then he explained the circumstances and Halter's face remained
grave.

"It's luck you come along when you did," he said, pointing to the slope. "They're going to make camp for the night."

"Looks like we're held here though," Dusty drawled.

"It looks like there'll be trouble here and at Fort Tucker," answered the scout. "When they hear they've still not got a leader the whole place'll blow apart at the seams."

"What're you meaning, friend?" asked Hogan grimly.

"You know how long the battalion's had to run without a commanding officer, with three green lieutenants in command?" drawled the scout, squatting on his heels. "They've done their best, but the men are getting slack, discipline's near on gone. Word gets out that new commander's dead you'll be lucky if there's a man left in the Fort come nightfall."

"Why was there such a delay in replacing the commanding officer?" asked Dusty.

"We lost the first man sent with the report, a fortnight went by before any of us thought anything about it. Got off Cragg with another message as soon as the shavetails realized the first hadn't got through. But by that time the damage was done."

All too well Dusty knew how quickly discipline could fade from men who were left without a strong leader. He could see the general slackening, the non-coms failing to hold control because of the lack of correct backing from the officers, in his imagination. The new commander at the Fort would need to be firm in his handling of the situation and he must get there in a hurry.

"Things started to get bad. The shavetails have managed to keep patrols out and stop the worst of the rushers getting through, but enough slip in and get out to make Eagle Catcher, he's the old man chief of the Sioux in this section, get riled and talk harsh," Halter went on. "Down in Shackville, 'bout a mile from the

Fort, the rushers are gathering. Word gets out that the new commanding officer's dead they'll go over the Tucker River and into the Black Hills—and mister, happen that many of them gets in every Sioux from here to the Canadian line'll paint for war. That old medicine-man, Sitting Bull'll start his dreaming again and we'll see the Sioux tribes, the Northern Cheyenne, the Blackfeet, all of them on the rampage.''

"Which's what the brass wants to avoid,'' Hogan said quietly. "They want to hold off this year, then next they plan to send in the biggest force that's been mustered since the War. Get all around the Sioux lands and close in, make them go into a reservation and stop at peace.''

None of the men spoke for a few moments. The soldiers were breaking out rations, sentries alert on each flank and watching the Sioux who kept enough men out to make sure there would be little chance of anyone slipping through their net. Over the rim fires flickered as the main body of the Indians prepared a meal. By now the sun had almost gone and soon night would descend on the land.

"Captain Fog,'' said Hogan quietly. "Would you stay on and take over the Fort until we can have a relief arranged?''

CHAPTER THREE

Dawn Attack

For a long moment Dusty Fog did not reply to Hogan's question. He stood with hands clasped behind his back and face bleak while Hogan, Mark and Halter watched him. Not one of them spoke, offering to help him make up his mind. Two of the men, Hogan and Halter, knew the seriousness of the situation even better than the third. Mark Knew Dusty, knew him as one Confederate officer knew another.

Dusty's eyes went to the company guidon which fluttered on its staff to one side of the camp, then to the blue sleeves of the uniform he wore.

"I was never so fond of your flag that I'd ride under it," he said quietly.

"The war ended ten years ago, Cap'n Fog," Hogan answered.

"Did it?" said Dusty. "And how about the southern boys like Bill Longley and Wes Hardin, did it end ten years ago for them?"

"No, or for a lot of folks. You know as well as I do that a thing like the War couldn't end and be forgotten like it never happened," replied Hogan. "It was less than a year after the war you rode south of the border into Mexico to fetch back Bushrod Sheldon.* He got fair treatment, and the men who came back with him."

Once more the silence dropped on the men. Dusty

---

* Told in *The Ysabel Kid*.

looked at Mark and the big blond man nodded gravely.

"You reckon I could get away with it?" asked Dusty.

Hogan waved a hand towards the soldiers who busied themselves at the task of feeding their horses or preparing a meal for themselves. The young man Dusty promoted to corporal appeared to be a natural in the way he handled the others and kept them working.

"There's not the one of them would say you're not an officer. And you fooled me, a man with twenty-eight years in the army."

"I'll do it on one condition," Dusty finally said.

"And that is?" asked the non-com.

"That you never forget, or try to get out of, the idea that I'm a captain in command of the Fort. I handle things the way I would if they were my troop and you take my orders as if I'd the full authority of the War Department behind me. Is that clear?"

"As clear as the waters of the River Shannon, which I've never seen but always heard were clear, sir," Hogan replied.

Dusty smiled. "All right, sergeant-major. You know what happens to people who impersonate officers, and to those who aid and abet them?"

"I've a fair idea, sir," grinned Hogan. "Sure I've never been in trouble through me entire career and I think me luck'll hold out for a bit longer."

"Do they know who'll be taking over at the Fort?" asked Mark.

"Sure," replied the scout. "The courier riding despatch between the posts brought word."

The men exchanged looks. Dusty saw a chance of their being detected before they even had a chance to do anything about squaring up the company and holding it together until a new commanding officer came from the regiment's headquarters.

"Who'd be likely to know van Druten?" he asked.

"Devil the few," replied Hogan. "Wasn't Dandy van Druten always the desk-warmer in Washington, where there's not been a man of the Fifteenth since the war?"

"They've all been with the regiment for at least five years, over at the Fort," agreed Halter. "I reckon you could get by as Dandy van Druten, Cap'n Fog. Who's going to think different when they see you ride in with the reinforcements and see me and the sergeant-major accepting you as van Druten?"

"Ain't but one thing to that," drawled the Kid sardonically, having come up in time to hear enough to know what was being planned. "We've got to get away from here first."

This brought all thoughts back to their present position. It did not seem worthwhile plotting what they might do when they reached the Fort, with a tough bunch of Hunkpapa Sioux out there, hidebound that the soldiers were staying where they were. All eyes went to Dusty and Hogan thought of how they might have been reacting if this man really was Dandy van Druten. The young officer would never have been able to pull the troop together in the way Dusty had on his arrival. Then the sergeant-major caught the glances Halter threw at the two Texans and realized the scout did not know them.

"Jim," he said. "This here's Mark Counter and the Ysabel Kid. Gents, get acquainted with Jim Halter."

"Thought that's who you might be," drawled Halter. "How're you aiming to put you two over at the Fort?"

"Lon can take over as scout and Mark ride with him," Dusty replied. "But like Lon said, we've got to get clear of that bunch first. What'll be their next play do you reckon, Jim?"

"Hold off until dawn for sure. Then they'll come in as soon as it's daylight to take us afore we're properly awake."

"Sure," agreed the Kid. "Only if that fails them they'll not be so all-fired eager to try again. If we could hit them hard enough on their first rush they might pull out."

"The Kid's right in that," Halter stated.

Dusty came to his feet and went to the side of the

wagons, peering through the fast coming night towards the surrounding country. He ignored the dead bodies of the Sioux, beyond making a mental note to warn the sentries to make sure they knew where each body in their area lay so as not to start shooting at a corpse in the darkness. His main attention went to the scrub oaks and rocks scattered around the area and in his mind's eye he pictured the land around the group of wagons.

Looking into the wagon he stood by, Dusty saw it to be filled with blankets and bales of clothing, replacements for the Fort's quartermaster's department. He guessed this to be a supply train, helping fill the Fort's stores for the forthcoming winter when the snow would cut it off from the rest of the world. In the wagons would be most of the things the soldiers at the Fort needed to survive in the Black Hills winter.

Turning, Dusty returned to the others. By now Hogan's iron hard frame had shaken off the effects of the blow on the head. He stood erect, peering around the camp to make sure all was under control and being done as Captain Fog wanted.

"What supplies have you?" asked Dusty.

"Ammunition, which I unloaded and stored in a trench between the horse lines. Clothing, general stores, saddlery, blacksmith's supplies, sir."

"Rope?"

"Three mile of it, in half-mile rolls, over there in the fourth wagon," Hogan answered.

This was as Dusty hoped, although he expected a vital commodity like rope would be included in the supply train. He could see the way the other men looked at him, and hid a grin as he saw the eager way in which Mark and the Kid watched his face. The time had long gone when he could fool them, or hide his emotions from either of his amigos. They knew, from his attitude and voice, that some plan had formed itself and he was going to pass it on to them. He expected that, though knowing him as they did, his idea might surprise even Mark and the Kid.

The young corporal, showing the sort of tact which along with his proven ability would carry him a long way as a career soldier, had caused a fire to be built at hand. With wood from the rawhide possum bellies under the wagons the men were making small fires near their posts and cooking food. The corporal started one for Dusty, then stood back, clearly awaiting orders.

"Corporal," Dusty said. "I didn't get your name."

"Dunbrowski, sir."

"You'd best hear this, it'll save me repeating myself."

The Kid had collected their coffee pot from the bedrolls and set it on the fire, filled with water from a butt on a wagon. He almost knocked it over as he spun around on hearing Dusty's plan. He, and all the others, stared at Dusty for the plan would call for skill, nerve and more than a little luck.

"It could work, given good men," drawled Halter.

"It's got to work, Jim," corrected Dusty. "Sure we can hold them off, but they'll whittle the command down slowly and we'll be using supplies needed for the fort. We've got to break that attack and break it hard. My way ought to do it."

The Kid grinned, his teeth showing white against his tanned skin in the firelight. "Comes to a real mean point, Dusty, there ain't no one but you, Jim, Mark and li'l ole me who'd be good enough in the dark to chance it."

"Going to need a few hands to tow all that rope though." Mark went on. "I reckon you thought out some way to run the rope out to us?"

Dusty nodded, turning to Dunbrowski. "That's your job, corporal. Take some men and break out one of those half-mile coils of rope. Get a crowbar from the blacksmith's stores and put it through the hole in the center of the coil, rest it on the sides of the wagon at a corner, so it can pay out."

"Yes, sir," replied Dunbrowski, his face showing he understood the order. He paused before going to obey the order. "Request permission to join the laying party, Cap'n, sir."

For a moment Dusty thought of refusing the permission and going himself. He saw the grin which flickered for a moment on Hogan's face and knew the reason. They both liked the spirit the young corporal showed. He did not volunteer for the dangerous mission because he thought doing so would impress his superior officers, but because he regarded it as part of his duty to go. Dusty promised himself that whatever the result of this affair, no matter how it ended for him, he would try and ensure Dunbrowski held the rank, for the young man was a soldier to the core and would make a good non-com.

"Permission granted," Dusty replied. "Take two men to assist in the paying-out party. You'll be in command of that detail tonight, sergeant-major."

"Yo!" Hogan answered; he would have liked to argue the order but knew better. Captain Fog was not the kind of officer a man argued orders with, not twice anyway.

"May I suggest the captain has lengths of cord cut to secure the rope in position at the right height?" put in Dunbrowski. "It might slip down if we don't."

"Good man," Dusty answered. "See to that. I'll have you in charge of that detail. You'll wait at the starting point with one man, then when the laying party return to you go around and secure the rope. See to it that every man has eaten in forty-five minutes, then allow the fires to die and have your detail standing by ready to move."

Dunbrowski went to attend to his duties. Watching the young man Dusty could see he'd made a good choice in the promotion, even though he'd no right to break the other soldier and give Dunbrowski the rank. There was the air of command about the young man, the way of a natural leader. The others obeyed him with a spring and willingness which the man Dusty broke could never get.

"There's a good soldier," Dusty remarked to Hogan as they settled down to a meal of jerked beef and hard-tack biscuits, washed down with hot coffee thick and strong enough to float an anvil. "You'll see he keeps his rank when the new post commander arrives?"

"That I will, sir," answered Hogan. "The army needs good non-coms, they're all that hold it together."

"I thought the officers had something to do with it," drawled Dusty, then glanced at the broken corporal who sat by the fire not worrying about his loss of rank by all appearances. "How about the one I broke?"

"Sure he wasn't never but a desk-warmer, sir," answered Hogan with a fighting soldier's contempt for administration personnel. "But young Dunbrowski, sir. He's such a natural he might be Irish."

With the meal finished and without needing to be told Dunbrowski gathered a quartet of muscular young soldiers and headed for one of the wagons. Dusty walked along to see his orders were obeyed. He stood back and allowed the corporal to get on with the work. Leaving the men to break out and cut the sacking from around a new bundle of rope Dunbrowski headed for the wagon with the blacksmith's stores and with the aid of a lantern found a stout crowbar. He did not come straight out of the wagon, but rooted around until he located a couple of large staples and a hammer. With these and the crowbar he headed back to the other wagon where his four men waited.

First the crowbar was passed through the hole in the center of the hard plaited Manila rope. Then it was lifted and the ends of the bar rested on the two sides of the wagon where they formed a corner, facing the open range. Next Dunbrowski placed a staple over each end of the bar and hammered it home, holding the bar in place so that the rope could be drawn off the coil. He made sure the rope ran smoothly, dismissed his men and reported to Dusty.

"We've nothing to do but wait now, corporal," Dusty remarked. "I'll have it placed on your record how well you handled the work. Set the men to cleaning their arms, then resupply with ammunition.''

"Yo!'' replied Dunbrowski and went to his work.

Watching Dunbrowski stride away, Dusty felt that they might pull off their wild masquerade. Clearly the young corporal did not doubt Dusty's right to give orders and accepted him as an officer. Dusty also saw that he could leave the routine duties in Dunbrowski's hands. Swiftly the corporal paraded the men, checked their ammunition and drew on the supply to replenish every man to his thirty-rounds quota. Then he set the men to cleaning their weapons.

Not until the arms were cleaned and the men fed did Dunbrowski relax. He joined Dusty's party at the central fire and taking a seat slid out the knife he carried in a boot-top sheath, took a piece of sandstone from his pocket and began to hone the blade.

"That's a fair-looking knife, *amigo,*'' said the Kid, looking at the weapon with some interest. "One of those made by Ames for the Dragoons in the Mexican War days ain't it?''

"Sure is, my pappy carried it down there.''

The Kid held out his hand and Dunbrowski held the knife hilt foremost to him. The Ames knife had been quite a weapon in its days, almost the equal of the bowie. The one held by the Kid was a good example of the type the Dragoons, and all who could get their hands on one, carried in the war with Mexico. With a blade eleven and three-quarters long the knife exceeded the Kid's bowie by a quarter of an inch. In width the bowie had an advantage, being two and a half inch at the guard to the Ames' inch and a half.

"Don't take to a spear-pointed knife myself,'' the Kid remarked, drawing his bowie to compare the weapons. "Nope, give me a clipped point any time. You can make a better backhand slash with the false edge of a clipped point. See you keep a good point on your knife. Most folks just sharpen the edge, but you need a good point in a fight.''

Taking back the knife Dunbrowski slipped it into his boot top and then settled himself on his side, pillowed his head on his arms and went to sleep. Dusty watched this with a smile flickering on his face.

"That's a real soldier," he said. "I'll take first watch, the rest of you catch what sleep you can."

Dusty allowed the fires to die down. Long after midnight, the camp all but in darkness, he woke his men. The Kid faded off into the darkness beyond the wagons and some time later returned as silently as he went.

"Quiet as the Llano Estacado at noon," he said quietly. "Head 'em up and point 'em out."

Hogan climbed into the wagon and took the end of the coil of rope, passing it to Mark and Halter as they stepped from the gap and into the hostile land beyond. They began to draw off the rope as they went through, followed by two men who would help tow the rope as more and more of it stretched behind Mark and Halter. Dunbrowski and another soldier followed them, each carrying several cut lengths of rope. They did not follow the first group beyond the nearest scrub oak. Here Mark and his party turned, the rope curling around the tree and following them. The Kid glided out and on his way, flanking the towing party, alert for any sign of the Sioux. He picked a careful way among the dead Indians which lay scattered on the ground from the earlier fighting, his knife in his hand, for he knew any defending of himself or the others could best be handled by cold steel.

At the first tree Dunbrowski stood, he kept one hand lightly on the passing rope feeling it running out steadily. Then his attention went to the body of a Sioux warrior which lay sprawled by a bush. He had not noticed it at first, then it caught his eye, laying flat on its belly with arms thrown out wide—only now the arms were not thrown wide and he could swear the dead Sioux had moved even closer, so that it now lay clear of the bush.

For a moment Dunbrowski watched the Indian but it made no movement. Or did it? Slowly it appeared to be

inching over the ground towards them. By Dunbrowski's side the other soldier fidgeted nervously, for
it was a nerve-racking business being out of the protec-
tive folds of the wagons. Dunbrowski hissed an order
for the soldier to stay still. His eyes never left the shape
on the ground, so slowly did it move that he might have
thought himself to be wrong. Only he knew he wasn't
wrong.

Dropping his hand towards the flap of his holster,
Dunbrowski prepared to draw and shoot. Then he
remembered Dusty's orders. Firearms must only be used
as a last resort. The shot would alert the Sioux and
might bring disaster to the rope-laying party. It would
certainly alarm the camp and some young sentry, his
nerves already on the jump, might throw lead wild to
the danger of Mark and the others. No, if he must deal
with the Sioux he had to do it in silence.

"Back down the rope to the wagon, Joe!" he
whispered urgently to the man at his side.

"I thought you sa——!"

"Do it, damn you!"

Silently the soldier obeyed and Dunbrowski slid the
Ames knife from his boot. Although it took all his will-
power, Dunbrowski kept standing with his back to
where he sensed the Sioux creeping towards him.

Hearing a soft movement behind him, Dunbrowski
sidestepped. Something shiny hissed by his shoulder and
buried into the tree tunk. Instantly he turned, driving
out his knife at the shape looming before him. The spear
point sank into flesh until he felt the hot gush of
stomach gases hit his hand and blood spurted over it. A
hand gripped his wrist and in trying to free it, he ripped
the knife through flesh. Soundlessly the shape fell away
from Dunbrowski's knife and went to the ground,
writhing at his feet.

"Nice moving, boy!"

The voice came floating from the darkness as gentle
and soft as a breath of wind and just as hard to pin
down as to its source. Dunbrowski came around fast,

the knife held ready for use. He saw nothing for a couple of seconds, then the Kid came into sight from the side where the corporal least expected him.

"There was one out here, Kid," he gasped.

"Yeah. Must have crawled down for water, or maybe to scout us," answered the Kid. "Reckon he either saw or heard you and came over for a look at what fool game you was playing. Thought to take him a coup."

Dunbrowski made no reply. Suddenly his stomach seemed to be heaving violently as he realized what he'd done. Yet he did not wish to be sick while the Kid was at hand, for that dark boy had reputedly killed more than one man with a knife. He would not think highly of a man who showed such a weak stomach that he fetched up because he'd dropped a Sioux warrior.

"Let it go, boy," drawled the Kid, resting a hand gently on the soldier's shoulder. "There's no shame in it."

With that the Kid faded off into the darkness once more, not wishing to embarrass Dunbrowski with his presence. The young corporal leaned against the tree and took the Kid's advice. He was in control of himself when he saw the rope-hauling party appear from the opposite direction to which they went on the way out. He helped Mark make the leading end of the rope secure to the tree, regulating the height carefully. Then with one of his lengths of cord he secured the rope to the correct height, lashing the cord into place to hold it there.

"Let's go, boy," said the Kid. "I'll come with you."

They made a circle of the camp, following the rope around and at the places where it curled around the trunk of a tree fastened it to the right height with the lengths of cord. By the time they'd finished the entire camp was surrounded at a distance varying according to where the nearest tree stood, from thirty to fifty yards by the rope. If it worked they would break the Sioux attack. If it failed the Sioux might take it as a sign the white man's medicine was bad and they'd gain heart by it.

The rope-laying party returned to the camp, slipping through the gap between the wagons and reporting to Dusty. The Kid entered last and threw a grin and wink at Dusty as Dunbrowski joined his captain, stood at a brace and reported.

"Everything set as ordered, sir."

"No trouble?" asked Dusty.

"I had to kill a Sioux scout. I did it silently."

"Bueno," drawled Dusty, then realized that Captain van Druten would hardly be likely to use Spanish words so casually. "You did well, corporal and I'll have it entered on your record."

"Orders for the morning, sir?" asked Dunbrowski, showing his pleasure at the words.

"Have the men standing to their posts at half an hour before first light. Make sure they take their places in silence."

"Yo!"

"Now catch some sleep," Dusty finished. "And you, sergeant-major."

"With all respect, sir," replied Hogan. "I'm rested. Would the captain get sleep? I'll wake him in time to stand-to."

"Thanks, I think I will," answered Dusty.

It hardly seemed to Dusty that he'd done more than closed his eyes when he felt a gentle hand shaking him. He opened his eyes and found Dunbrowski kneeling beside him holding a mug of coffee.

"The sergeant-major told me to waken you, sir," he said. "Company is fallen in as you ordered. There is some activity among the Sioux but no sign of an attack so far."

"My compliments to the sergeant-major," Dusty replied, taking the mug. "I want one man with a repeater at each flank. The three scouts to take north, south and east flanks. I'll be at the west."

"Yo!" Dunbrowski answered and shot away to deliver the order. Dusty sat up and looked the camp over. In the east the sky bore just the faintest lightening which would herald the new day. Soon would be the time of the attack, the time when the plan would either succeed or fail.

Finishing his coffee Dusty watched his orders being obeyed. Slowly the grey of dawn improved, the trees around the camp showed clearly and the rest of the area came gradually into view as the day became lighter.

"Here they come!"

The Kid, watching the slopes, gave a warning shout. The Hunkpapa came racing their horses down at what should have been a camp slow-witted and stiff with sleep or by lack of it.

They came fast, riding their war ponies in a wild rush which should smash down the defenders and give the victorious warriors loot and coups. Too late the charging braves saw the rope strung around the camp. The horses smashed into it, piling over and going down. Pandemonium reigned among the attacking braves, the first were thrown from their horses, others tried to stop their racing war ponies before they hit the rope.

"Fire at random!" Dusty roared. "Pour it on!"

From all around the wagons the guns crashed out, Springfields bellowing in with the sharper, rapid cracks of repeating rifles and the whiplash bark of Dusty's carbine. The Sioux found themselves caught in a withering and murderous fire, thrown into confusion by the failure of their rush.

Brave heart never met with such adversity without deciding it was long gone time to head for home. The attack on the soldier-coats had been met all the way with bad medicine. This final attack proved the gods were not with the raiding party.

A war-bonnet chief gave a yell, swinging his horse just in time to avoid the medicine-breaking rope. He raised his lance over his head and screamed out something in Hunkpapa tongue. The rest changed their tactics. The wounded were scooped up, men unhorsed by the rope bounded on to riderless mounts or behind their lodge brothers. Then they were gone, streaming up the slopes away from the ill-fated oblong of wagons which should have been easy prey and yet which broke their medicine.

For a moment the soldiers watched the Sioux go. Then word that the attack had ended passed from mouth to mouth. The recruits began to cheer, waving their hats in the air, showing excitement at their first taste of victorious combat.

Dusty rested his carbine against the wagon side and looked to where the sergeant-major ran towards him.

"We did them, sir," Hogan said. "It worked!"

"Parade the men," Dusty replied. "Dunbrowski, a burial detail for our dead. Hogan, have a meal prepared. Get that rope gathered in, it's on the quartermaster's list and he'll want it delivered to him. Come on, man. We haven't all day to waste."

With a salute Hogan turned and headed to begin his duties. He did not even think that Dusty shouldn't be giving orders in such a tone. The agreement made was that Dusty received the same courtesy as would be given to the real officer. Hogan grinned to himself. It would be Lord help any man who didn't render the correct respect to Captain Dusty Fog.

"Sergeant-major!" Dusty roared. "I want to be ready to roll in two hours' time. See to it!"

"You heard the captain?" Hogan bellowed at the soldiers as they fell in before him, standing in two files. "Corporal Dunbrowski, stables detail, water the horses."

Dusty stood by watching the bustle of the camp. He still did not know if he was doing the right thing in taking over like this. One thing he did know. To the best of his ability he aimed to take over that leaderless and demoralized battalion and shake it into shape, or kill half of the blue-belly soldiers trying.

CHAPTER FOUR

Fort Tucker

Perched on the Dakota plains, Fort Tucker proved to be a collection of wooden cabins which housed the battalion and such families as followed their men west. A wall, far too low to be called a palisade, but offering some slight protection to a defender, surrounded the area. Each face of the wall's square had a gate in it; the main entrance facing east, large enough for wagons to enter and covered by the guard-house. The north gate led to Madlarn's sutler's post; the south to Shacktown, a mushroom village where rushers waited for a chance to slip across the Belle Pourche River into the Black Hills; while the last gate opened on the rolling plains.

At the main gate of the Fort a soldier stood on what might have been termed sentry by someone not versed with military ideas. He leaned his shoulder against the wall, a piece of straw in his mouth and his Springfield carbine resting by his side. Nor did he offer to straighten and do any of the things a sentry should by orders do when a party approached. He studied them, deciding they must be the new recruits and officer. So he raised his left hand in a cheery greeting rather than anything resembling a salute.

Dusty flung his paint's reins to Dunbrowski, who rode as guidon carrier at his side. Then he came down from the military saddle and stepped forward. His left hand swung, knocking the straw from the soldier's mouth. His right hand bunched into the amazed man's shirt front and hauled him close. With his face scant inches from the soldier's and eyes glowing with fury Dusty studied the other for a moment.

"Do you know me?" he asked, thrusting the man backwards with the ease of brushing off a fly.

"N-nope——" gulped the thoroughly startled soldier. "N-no, sir."

The latter came when he saw Dusty's brows knit at the omission of the word, "sir" at his first "nope."

"Then why in hell didn't you halt me and the troop, salute my rank and call out the sergeant of the guard?"

Coming to a smarter brace than he'd managed for a few weeks the soldier stood rigid. Something warned him to give only one answer.

"No excuse, sir."

"Sergeant-major!" barked Dusty over his shoulder. "Find this man a week's hard work to remind him of his duties!"

"Yo!" came Hogan's reply.

For all that the burly sergeant-major could hardly hide a smile which flickered across his face. The slight doubt he'd held that Dusty might not be able to handle the deal left him. From the look of that soldier he not only took Dusty for a U.S. cavalry officer but suspected he'd tangled with the Provost-Marshal of the command.

"And you," Dusty went on, giving his attention to the man who by a series of remarkable muscular contortions had managed to get his carbine to the shoulder without breaking his brace. "Listen to me with both your ears. Spread this among your bunkies. The next man who fails to respect my rank'll go into the cells and, by God, will wish he'd never been born! Call out the sergeant of the guard."

It took the sentry three shouts to bring the guard commander from his post in the guardhouse. He proved to be an unshaven and untidy looking corporal and came forward at a trot, fastening his weapon belt as he ran. Halting before Dusty the corporal threw up a ragged salute.

For a moment Dusty did not speak, just looked the corporal over.

"At ease, Corporal," he said, his voice so cold it almost brought a shiver to the non-com's campaign toughened hide. "Attention, private. You're relieved of rank and duty. Hogan, assign this man to latrine detail, it appears to be all he's fit for."

The corporal's mouth dropped open. He'd been in the army long enough to know a captain, especially one with the rank of fort commander, could reduce him to the ranks. He'd never believed one would do it in so few words, although he had the fairness of mind to admit he derserved it for his appearance and neglect of duty.

"You heard the captain, soldier," said Hogan, dismounting and walking forward. "Get those bars from your sleeves and report to me in the office in twenty minutes."

All too well Hogan knew there could be no hesitation in the way he or Dusty acted. He knew the corporal, a good enough soldier, but like most of the other ranks of the army, not a well-educated man. Such fell easily into boredom and forgot the strict training driven into them unless led by a firm hand. He could see the Fort needed that firm hand on it quickly before it burst apart at the seams. The young lieutenants did not have the knowledge or experience to handle rough campaign hardened veterans like this battalion and slowly it began to rot away.

"Dunbrowski, take over as corporal of the guard," Dusty went on. "Hogan, with me."

The remainder of the main-gate guard were settled down for a leisurely afternoon, lazing around the front part of the building. Suddenly the door burst open and a tornado hit them. Dusty's tongue, learned under a master of vituperation in the Confederate Army, matured handling cowhands on range work and trail drive, finished in the wild cattle towns, lashed the men, throbbing with fury. For five minutes without stop he told the guard what he thought of it, its morals, ancestors and descendants, never repeating himself and drawing on every dreg of his years of learning.

"Now get to your quarters and return in stable fatigue," he finished. "I'm putting a new guard in and they're not coming into this hawg-pen. I want this place so clean I could bring the colonel's lady in and let her eat her food off the boards. Move!"

The guard scattered and headed for the barrack blocks. A pair of them headed across the square on the double and one looked at the other.

"That's Dandy van Druten, that was," he said. "Wowee! We had a good time for the past few weeks, James me boy. But it's over now."

"Least we're off duty and can have a night at Madlarm's," answered James. "Which same I reckon we're going to need it."

"And aren't going to get it. I've a nasty idea that captain's going to keep folks too busy for them to go any place at all."

Standing on the porch Dusty watched the soldiers depart. He happened to look towards where Mark and the Kid sat to one side of the troop. Mark's face held a grin and his eye dropped in a wink. Jim Halter was not with the men, for Dusty insisted they sent him to regimental headquarters with a message telling what had happened and what they planned to do. This might not help in case of a court martial for Hogan and Dusty, but might ease the sentence on the big non-com. It had been a decision reached on the night after the fight with the Sioux. Dusty guessed he might be recognized and sending the letter could help partly exculpate them.

Dusty did not have time to waste thinking about his actions, the rights and wrongs of his decision. There was much to do, organizing that he must attend to even before he began to shake the Fort up.

"Dunbrowski, tell off a guard detail from your men. Hogan, relieve every sentry in the camp of his duty, have them all report to help police the guardhouse and area. Dunbrowski, I'll send one of the Fort sergeants to acquaint you with your orders as soon as I can. Until then carry on as you would under the same circumstances with the regiment."

With that Dusty headed for the officers' quarters. The wagons had rolled into the Fort but for all the notice anybody took they might have not been within a hundred miles of it. The large square lay empty and deserted, not a soul stirred on it. Behind the barrack cabins Dusty could hear children laughing and playing but not a sign of life could he see.

A most annoyed Dusty reached officers' country, the block in which he and the three lieutenants lived. No longer did Dusty think of himself as an impostor, holding down his job until a replacement came. He felt just as he would have if he arrived as the genuine fort commander.

In the old days when he rode as captain in command of Troop "C" Texas Light Cavalry, if the word went out, "Dusty's on the warpath," people made themsleves scarce or made damned sure they gave full attention to their military duties. By the time he'd done with this lot they'd be just the same.

Quite a sight greeted Dusty's eyes as he passed an open door marked with a card announcing the officer of the day was inside and for people to knock and wait. Dusty neither knocked nor waited, but stepped inside.

Stretched flat on his back; a towel over his eyes, a tartan shirt, and pair of Crow moccasins on his feet at odds with his yellow striped cavalry trousers; at peace with the world lay First-Lieutenant Frank Gilbey. He felt pleasantly at ease for this was Saturday afternoon and by allowing the men to relax he could forget the worries of trying to hold the battalion together until Monday, by which time the new commander should be on hand. Then he could take a week's well deserved furlough to go hunting, see if he could nail a good proghorn buck to send for his father's collection of game heads.

Gilbey did not offer to open his eyes when he heard someone enter the room, or remove the towel. He expected it would be his striker come to clean his boots and gear, so settled back to relax for a couple more seconds. They were the last seconds of relaxation coming his way for some time.

"May I ask just what the hell you are, mister?" asked a voice which although holding a southern drawl had all the hard-bitten toughness of a strict disciplinarian senior officer.

Jerking away the towel Gilbert studied the small man in the travel-stained captain's uniform for a moment, then came to his feet with a welcoming smile.

"Gilbey, sir. First-Lieutenant, officer of the day."

Somehow Frank Gilbey got the impression that his words did not meet with the newcomer's approval. A pair of cold grey eyes studied him from head to foot, taking in his side-whiskers and moustache, worn to make him look older, his tartan shirt, then dropping to the moccasins.

"You're sure that's who you are, mister?" asked Dusty savagely. "You're not some trail-end town mac blacksmithing on the calico cats?"

Gilbey frowned. He did not stop to wonder where a desk warmer from the east, like this Dandy van Druten, might know such terms as mac for pimp, blacksmithing used to describe pimp's living on the earnings of a calico cat, or prostitute. All he knew was he'd been insulted.

"Here, easy——!" he began.

"Easy, mister!" roared Dusty in a tone which took Gilbey back to the days where he was a raw plebe at the West Point. It slammed a brace into his shoulders and warned him that, no matter what he'd heard of Dandy van Druten, this man would stand for no laxness in military etiquette. "Have you forgotten your training. You salute a senior officer and you address him as sir. Why are you out of uniform?"

"No excuse, sir."

While leaving a lot unexplained the reply was the only one Gilbey could make under the circumstances. His instincts and good sense warned him not to state truthfully that he had been taking advantage of his temporary position as post commander to relax. He'd been in command ever since Major Lingley died and suddenly he saw how he'd missed his chance. This was not entirely true. He'd known a new post commander would be along and tried to hold things together. On hearing Dandy van Druten would be the next commander he let things slip, for he knew the other would never acknowledge his junior officers' abillity lest it detract from his own record.

Gilbey stood rigid at a brace with the cold unfriendly eyes on his face. A thought puzzled him, something about Dandy van Druten, yet he could not tie it. It came almost as a relief when Dusty spoke again, although one might term it the relief at having a sore throat after toothache.

"Perhaps a week as officer of the day might remind you of your duties, mister," Dusty snapped. "You will report in uniform, with the other officers, to my office in fifteen minutes. In uniform, mister!"

With that Dusty took Dandy van Druten's watch from his tunic pocket and looked at it, closed the case and walked out of the room. For a long moment Gilbey stood and watched the open door. Then slowly he wiped his brows. The point of that glance taken at the watch did not escape Gilbey. Fifteen minutes he had and if he took more he'd wish he did not.

"Wow!" he gasped, heading for the next room. "That Dandy van Druten's a mean one. But, by all that's holy, he's a soldier and he'll shake the battalion together one way or another."

In the next room Second-Lieutenant Farrow slept in peace, a slim, wiry and cheery youngster. He jerked erect as Gilbey shook him, gasping out a demand to know what all the excitement was for.

"He's here," Gilbey answered. "We've got fifteen minutes to get into number one uniform and report to his office. Where's Card?"

"Took Joanna for a ride to see if they could scáre up a mess of fool-hens," answered Farrow.

Gilbey clasped a hand to his forehead. "No!" he groaned. "I'll never get off officer of the day."

Before Farrow could ask questions which boiled in his mind Gilbey dashed back to his own room and started to dig out his best field uniform. Farrow came to the door.

"Hey, what's all the fuss?"

"The fuss, Jimmy boy," snapped Gilbey, "is that Captain van Druten wants to see us in his office in about eleven minutes and I for one don't aim to be late or untidy. Now get the hell out of here and leave me to change."

Farrow turned, scratched his head. Then he realized what Gilbey had said. If Frank Gilbey was jumping like a flea on a griddle it would be as well to hop to the music. He dashed into his own room and jerked open his foot-locker ready to change.

Even in the short time since entering the officers' quarters Dusty found a change in the square. Hogan acted as he would if Dusty really commanded the troop, which meant he did not 'waste time. From the men in camp he'd organized a detail to off-load, under guard, a large, stout and well locked iron chest from one wagon. In this chest lay the pay for the battalion for the next month. The other wagons were parked behind the buildings, their teams being cared for. Men scattered and scurried about and from the guardhouse came the sound of the scrubbing brushes working on wood.

"I'll be in my office if you want me, Hogan," Dusty said. "Bring the payroll in when you're able."

"Yo!" Hogan replied, for the box was made to make easy transport a slow and tedious matter.

To one side of the orderly room, with a door opening on to the square as well as in the office, lay the fort commander's office. Dusty turned the handle and stepped in. He shoved the door closed and stepped forward. A soft footfall came behind him and two hands came around, warm, soft hands, covering his eyes and a woman's voice said:

"Guess who, Dandy?"

Gently Dusty removed the hands then turned. The woman gasped and staggered back a couple of steps, her face reddening in a blush as she gasped, "You're not Dandy van Druten!"

"No, ma'am," Dusty replied. "What're you doing in my office?"

He studied the woman. She was not tall, five foot two at most, with a rich plump little figure and a cheap gingham dress cut a trifle more daringly than one might expect. Her hair had a mousey brown tint and her face was passable pretty but her eyes were inviting, bold, teasing and her lips looked ready to smile, or laugh encouragingly at any man she saw.

"But—but I——we——!" she began.

Not only did Dusty's office have a front door to the square and party door to the orderly room, there was a third entrance at the rear, leading to his quarters instead of his having to go around the front. This third door suddenly burst open and a red-faced sergeant burst in. He stopped just inside the door, a middle-sized man with the light spring of a sword fighter in his poise, the sabre in his hand gripped like its owner knew how to handle it, the blade bare. To Dusty's eyes the man was a tough professional non-com and not the kind to burst unannounced into the office of his commanding officer without the stress of some emotion.

On recalling his greeting as he entered the office Dusty could guess what the emotion might be.

For a couple of seconds the sergeant, woman and Dusty stood without a word.

"Get out of here, Noreen," said the sergeant.

"Sergeant!" snapped Dusty, then heard a knock and Hogan asked if he could come in. "Wait!" Dusty barked and looked at the sergeant as the woman almost ran by him to the door. "I'd like——"

"You're not Dan—Captain van Druten, sir."

"Did I say I was?"

"No—no, sir. But orders reached us that——"

"Does the Department of the Interior inform *you* if they make a change of orders, Sergeant?" snapped Dusty. "Why did your wife, I take it she is your wife, come in here just now?"

Smartly, too smartly for a frontier trained soldier, the sergeant came to a brace and brought his sabre up in a salute.

"No excuse, sir."

A half smile flickered across Dusty's face and went before the sergeant could see or put meaning to it. Everybody in Fort Tucker appeared to have no excuse for their conduct.

"Your name, Sergeant?"

"Kallan, sir. Acting as D.I. for the battalion."

"You'll have a chance to show me how well you've done your work in the morning, Kallan. In future don't be in such a hurry to see me that you come from sabre practice without sheathing your weapon. Open the door and allow Sergeant-major Hogan to come in."

The sergeant rested his sabre against the wall and stepped forward, saluting. "I'd like to apologize for my wife's behav——"

"If the lady is industrious enough to get here first and try to arrange for my washing to augment her allowance it's to be commended, not apologized over. How did she get in?"

"One key'll open every lock in the fort, sir. But my wife——"

Dusty swung to face the man. "The explanation I gave will be all we need say. But, Sergeant, happen you hope to hold those bars, when I tell you to do anything, be it impossible, or as easy as opening a door, I expect you to start on it without hesitation."

Kallan headed for the door fast, jerking it open and Hogan entered, throwing a glance at him.

"Howdy, Ted," he greeted, looking worried. "I sure

didn't know you'd come out to Tucker.''

"Kraus took down with the fever and I filled in his place," Kallan replied, but he still looked puzzled.

At any moment he would ask, in a furtive whisper, who the new officer might be, thought Dusty, and took steps to avoid this until he'd time to discover more about the Kallan family.

"Would you gentlemen mind discussing old home week in your quarters?" he barked. "I'd prefer to have my office to myself."

Stiffening into a brace and throwing salutes along with their apologies like two non-coms rebuked by their commanding officer, the two men gave their attention to watching the heavy payroll box moved into the office. The previous box, empty now except for company funds, stood to one side of the roof and would return to the Regiment's headquarters with the supply wagons.

By the time the box had been placed against the inner wall of the building and the carrying detail marched out of the room Dusty received two of his three officers, both a trifle red in the face from the rush to make themselves smart and presentable, their strikers both being off the post.

Duty sat at the commanding officer's desk as the two officers entered. He looked at Hogan and Kallan, standing in the corner of the room. "Sergeant-major, take a detail and move my belongings into my quarters. Sergeant Kallan, go to the guardhouse and tell the corporal of the guard his duties, then take him around the sentry posts."

"Yo!" replied Kallan, the only answer he could make under the circumstances. He wished he could go with Hogan and solve the mystery of this captain who clearly was not Dandy van Druten. This way he would be kept busy for some time and not have a chance to see Hogan until finished with the duty.

"Now, gentlemen," Dusty said quietly, looking at the two officers. "May I ask what's happening at this post?"

"We are carrying out our orders, sir, maintaining patrols with the intention of keeping rushers——" began Gilbey.

"I understood there were three officers on the post, Mr. Gilbey," Dusty interrupted. "Or do your services render you worth two?"

"Second-Lieutenant Cardon is escorting Joanna on a hunting trip, sir," put in Jarrow.

"Mister," Dusty answered dryly. "I've no doubt you are a man of some talent and ability, although for the moment both escape me. But I'm only human, not a mind reader. Who might Joanna be?"

"Major Lingley's daughter, sir," Gilbey put in, throwing a warning glance at Jarrow. "She stayed at the post awaiting a proper escort to take her back to headquarters."

"Thank you, Mr. Gilbey. Now, the state of the Fort is far from good enough."

Gilbey stiffened slightly. "I assume full responsibility as senior officer, sir."

"Very well, mister."

With any other answer Gilbey would have found Dusty showing a very different attitude. He deserved some commendation for the way he assumed the full blame for the condition of the Fort, even though it might cause him to face court martial and ruin. He'd stood like a man and prepared to take his medicine.

A smile came to Dusty's lips and his eyes lost the hard grim look with which he first studied them.

"Youth and inexperience can be classed as extenuating circumstances for some things, mister—once. Our problem now is how to get our command back to its former standards!"

In those words Dusty made another two friends, two more of the many who would gladly side the Rio Hondo gun-wizard in anything he planned without caring what the circumstances might be. Neither missed the way he referred to the battalion as their command. Yet Dandy van Druten had never been noted, from what they'd heard of him, as a man who would give his juniors credit for doing more than living and breathing. They were beginning to change their minds about him.

Neither lieutenant failed to notice as they walked through the camp to the office how many people scurried about and got on with their work. The men they saw already showed something of the liveliness which Major Lingley's command instilled in them and they worked with a will. Already word spread around the Fort of Dusty's actions on arrival. Such non-coms as were still on post studied their own chevrons and set their men to work with gusto. The men heard, from the new recruits, highly embroidered stories of Dusty's vigorous leadership and strict expectance that any order he gave be instantly obeyed, if not even quicker than that. So everybody now moved with a will and purpose, all except those lucky enough to be off post and out of the way of the new commanding officer.

"Request permission to speak alone with the captain," Gilbey said.

"Granted," replied Dusty. "You're dismissed, Mr. Jarrow. Have assembly sounded in ten minutes."

"Yo!" ejaculated Jarrow, saluting and taking a rapid departure.

"They never change, do they?" smiled Dusty as the door closed on Jarrow.

"Who, sir?"

"Young shavetails. Never saw one yet who wouldn't hightail it out of his commanding officer's way. Have a chair, Mr. Gilbey."

"A kind of natural protection, sir," Gilbey answered, a little pride in his tone that his captain should regard him as superior in intelligence and rank to at least one person in the world. "I broke a sergeant and ordered him for court martial on a charge of insolence, sir."

"You have the papers on the case?"

"Er—no, sir. After I broke him—well——"

"Start from the beginning, mister, please. I'm not a mind reader, as I told Mr. Jarrow."

"The sergeant's name is Magoon, sir. He's a typical combat soldier. Put him anywhere he can't be out fighting Indians and he's back to private in days. He was my company sergeant and a good man. I'm afraid we both became a little heated over a party of rushers who slipped by us and into the Black Hills."

"He was sober at the time?"

"Yes, sir," answered Gilbey. "We both were, Magoon never drinks when he's on duty. However, I broke him and he made a remark, which I'll admit I asked for, and I ordered him to await return to Regimental headquarters for court martial."

"Your problem, mister?" asked Dusty.

"He's a good soldier, sir, and a first-class three bar. Our hold on the men was weakened just that much when I broke him. I was at fault and now——"

"You want me to refuse to approve the court martial and try to give him back his rank without endangering discipline?"

"Yes, sir."

Dusty rose and paced the room with his hands clasped behind him. He came to a halt at his desk and looked at Gilbey but his eyes held a twinkle.

"I think it was General Hardin who said the main purpose of a lieutenant was to provide problems for his seniors to solve. I'll do what I can," he remarked. "Now to the matter of the Fort."

Sitting at the desk facing Gilbey, Dusty got down to the business of his taking over the Fort. Outside he heard the notes of a bugle before they'd had a chance to do much. Assembly sounded and they shoved their chairs back to get to their feet. Gilbey opened the door and they stepped out. Jarrow stood waiting, looking worried and as he looked towards the parade square Dusty saw why.

CHAPTER FIVE

Magoon Meets His Hero

For a long five seconds Dusty studied the men on the parade square before him. The recruits, not having been allocated to their companies yet, stood to one side. The remaining men, under their sergeants, stood in the three company blocks. Dusty knew each company held a strength of thirty men instead of the regulation fifty. This did not surprise him, for most regiments found themselves under strength; the thirty recruits were here to build up the company numbers, not make another company.

However, standing in the three blocks of the "A", "B" and "C" companies were less than half of their strength. Duty estimated almost fifty men out of ninety were not on parade.

With fingertips tapping lightly on his sides, Dusty turned to Gilbey. "Well, mister?" he said.

"They're most likely off the post, sir," put in Jarrow, hopping along with the grace of a club-footed moose where angels and Frank Gilbey would fear to tread. "Down to the sutler's and—well, maybe they didn't hear the call, sir."

The latter part of his words came to a lame halt as he realized he hadn't exactly helped the situation in any way. He stiffened into a brace and Gilbey threw a withering look at him.

"You'd suggest we sent the bugler down to blow the

call inside, mister?'' asked Dusty in a quiet growl which reminded Jarrow unpleasantly of instructors at West Point just before they handed out pack drill or extra guard detail. ''Do it that way and they might decide to come along and do a bit of soldiering.''

''No, sir. I'll go and——''

''No, mister, *I'll* go!'' snapped Dusty. ''Mr. Gilbey, I want those supply wagons emptied before night, so put the men to it. I also want the names of every man on this working detail.''

Acknowledging the salute, Dusty turned on his heel and walked away. Gilbey mopped his brow. ''Come on, Jimmy,'' he said. ''Let's make a start. And another thing, unless you want to wind up helping me with my week of officer of the day you want to restrict your conversation with Captain van Druten to three words. Yes, sir and no, sir. But for your own sake get them in the right places.''

Hogan fell in alongside Dusty as the small Texan headed for the west gate and the post sutler's store.

''Your amigos put your horses and theirs in the officers' stables, sir. I fixed for them to bunk with the officers. They've gone along to the sutler's to get tobacco and cigarette papers.''

''*Bueno*,'' Dusty replied. ''How's it going?''

''Slasher Kallan'll be the hard part. He was at the Point when van Druten did his time. I didn't know he was with this battalion.''

''Why'd he leave the Point?''

Hogan did not reply for a moment, he looked rather embarrassed at the words. ''Nobody knows for sure. They moved a tolerable lot of staff personnel out at the same time, put it down to general turnover. Only Slasher Kallan had been the best D.I. and sabre instructor they'd had and his sort don't usually get affected by general turnover. Beyond that, sir, I know nothing.''

''You didn't like van Druten?'' asked Dusty.

"Devil the few who did, sir."

"And was he any way connected with Kallan?"

"Like I said, I know nothing. Only vague rumors. True or not I can't say and don't want to try."

They strode on again with Dusty returning the salutes of such men as they passed, for his words on the subject were relayed around the fort. He worked the problem out in his mind.

"We're going to need a change of plan, friend. I'm going to have to come out flat-footed and use my own name. Is that story about General Grant offering me a commission in the Union Army after the war ended* known to many folks?"

"There's quite a few have heard it. We've a sergeant out here, Reb we call him, Milton Granger's his name rode under Hood in the War. He's told enough of us about it."

"Then that's how we'll play it. We'll let things ride that way, give out my name and leave it that folks allow I've taken on the General's offer."

"It might raise some confusion, sir. The recruits have been calling you van Druten," Hogan pointed out.

"Then we'll unconfuse them. You'll put it out that I reckoned everybody'd know my name and didn't bother to announce the change of orders."

By this time they'd reached the gate leading to the post sutler's store and the sentry came to attention, fetching up his carbine smartly. Hogan threw a look at the building, listening to the drunken laughter and shouts which came from it. He knew what Dusty aimed to do.

"Need me along, sir?" he asked hopefully, for he wished to see how, not if, Dusty handled the matter.

"Not this time. I'll want to see all officers and sergeants as soon as I'm through in here."

Leaving Hogan to attend to his orders Dusty stepped

* Told in *The Fastest Gun in Texas*, J. T. Edson.

through the gate, giving a smart salute in return to the sentry's drill square movements with his Springfield carbine. Then with purposeful strides Dusty headed for the post sutler's store.

After attending to their own and Dusty's horses and leaving them in the officers' stables Mark and the Kid headed for the orderly room to find Dusty busy. Hogan told them to take their bedrolls to the spare room in the officers' quarters as they classed as Dusty's guests rather than scouts. With this done and being very short of smoking material they headed for the post sutler's store.

Set in a large one-storey log building the store contained, in a quarter of its length, an establishment where a variety of goods could be bought and even more ordered through the wish books which lay on the counter, catalogues from various mail order houses. The remaining three-quarters of the bulding, since Karl Madlarn took over, became a saloon, rest home, sporting house for the soldiers. It also, in the opinion of the experienced sergeants, provided a brewing ground for discord and dissent, a center of anarchy and near mutiny, for Madlarn encouraged the men to drink when they should be working, which made a good start to wrecking the discipline of the battalion.

On entering the saloon end Mark and the Kid knew they'd best stay a while. The room had a large number of soldiers sitting around tables, drinking, gambling, talking or singing. They were not such soldiers as would meet Dusty's approval, for not one had a clean uniform and few appeared to have shaved that morning or for a few days. Mark and the Kid also knew the *amigo* would come alone to handle the matter and so should stay a while in case he needed a hand.

"Ole Dusty sure ain't going to be happy about this lot," drawled Mark as they took their beers to a table by the wall and sat down.

"He surely ain't," answered the Kid with a grin.

"These Yankee blue-bellies are headed for real trouble and soon."

"That's Madlarn, I'd say," Mark went on, indicating a tall, florid faced man who moved around the room.

"Likely," agreed the Kid.

The guess did not have much chance of failing for the florid faced man was a civilian and wore the clothes of a boss, not a worker. He might have been termed handsome in some places, sporting the latest fashion in moustaches and side-whiskers and with hair slicked down by liberal dosage of bay rum, Madlarn looked like a typical city slicker. His eastern style suit fitted well and though he might be powerful he'd run to fat after the way of a man who took little exercise and spent most of his time sitting at a card table.

At this moment Madlarn was not seated at a card table. He passed among his guests dispensing cheerful words and laughing at coarse replies. Behind the bar the two bartenders, his sole employees, served drinks. They were a pair of big, hefty, brutal-looking men who looked to have learned their trade in some raw Barbary Coast tavern where a customer was likely to wake up after one drink and find himself on a clipper ship headed for China.

"They tell me your new boss's here, boys," Madlarn said, with a broad grin on his face. "I reckon you'll soon show him who's the real bosses of Fort Tucker."

There came a muttered growl of agreement from the men at the words. Discipline, long enough lacking to have almost gone from the heads of a lot of the soldiers, would need to be thrust home hard and fast. Unless Dusty did it, or if he failed to do it fast, there'd be mutiny and worse at Fort Tucker.

The notes of assembly sounded, coming to the ears of the celebrating soldiers. Some of them, in fact most, started to thrust back their chairs but Madlarn went among them like a hostess trying to revive interest in a flagging party. He poured drinks and shoved men into their seats.

"Settle down, boys," he said. "Shucks, it's Saturday afternoon. You show him that you know your rights as fighting soldiers. Go on, finish your drinks." He came to halt at one table where two corporals and a big, burly private still remained on their feet. It was to the private he spoke. "Sit down, Paddy. Didn't they bust you at the Fort and for no reason. You show these boys you know your rights."

Mark and the Kid studied the big man, noting the darker patches on his sleeves where three chevrons had been for some considerable time and only recently removed. In size and heft he all but equalled Mark, although without the trimming down at the waist. His close-cropped red hair framed a face which proclaimed his nationality as clearly as if it were painted emerald green and had Ireland tattooed across the forehead.

"That big hombre's got a tolerable amount of pull," the Kid said, nodding to the burly ex-sergeant.

Watching the way other men sat and relaxed when Magoon took his seat once more, Mark agreed with the Kid. Mark could guess at the big Irishman's action. Magoon wished to see how the new fort commander acted, for a man must always prove himself before Paddy Magoon accepted him.

Talk welled up again, with Madlarn passing among the crowd to keep up the feeling that they were within their rights. Magoon sat down once more, talking with the two oldish, tough-looking corporals in a low voice. The minutes crawled by and Madlarn stood in the center of the room. He did not see the door open behind him as he announced:

"There you are, boys. He knows you're men who stand up for your rights. He's not blown assembly again."

Somehow Madlarn got the idea his words did not

quite make the impression he wanted. Talk died away
throughout the room, men seemed to be staring towards
the door in a most unnatural and uneasy manner. A
glance taken in the mirror told Madlarn why.

Dusty Fog stood just inside the door, his hands
tucked into his waist belt, his captain's bars glinting in
the light of the room. For a long moment he stood
there, then stepped forward to halt just before Madlarn.
He turned and looked at the men, the disgust and anger
in his eyes making them look any place but at him.

"All right, you goldbricks," he said. "Out!"

A big, burly soldier of Germanic origin pushed himself to his feet. He'd managed to raise a fair head of
steam on the raw whisky sold by Madlarn and so leaned
on the table, one palm against it, the other on top of a
whisky bottle, giving the necessary support to stand
erect.

"This is not right," he began. "Wha——"

Which was as far as he got, it having taken Dusty just
that long to reach him. Dusty's left hand came around,
slapping the bottle from under the man's palm and
throwing him right off balance so his jaw came forward.
Knotted into a hard first Dusty's right hand drove up to
connect with the German's thrust out jaw. The blow
cracked like a pair of king-sized billiard balls coming
together and the soldier snapped erect, crashed back
into his chair, shattered it under his weight and landed
flat on his back.

Mark winced in sympathy as he saw the blow land.
Once, in a wild burst of horseplay, at the OD Connected
he'd walked into one of Dusty's punches, thrown at
much less power than the one just landed. His jaw ached
for a day after it and so he didn't reckon the big German
would feel like eating any hard food for a few meals to
come.

The punch made an impression on quite a number of
people. At his table big Paddy Magoon let out a sigh

and said reverently, "Now there's a real Irishman's punch, darlin's."

Stepping towards Dusty, Madlarn snarled out. "You can't stop these soldiers having their rights!"

Then he proceeded to make a fool mistake. Mark and the Kid could have warned him not to try his next move. He shot out his hand to catch Dusty's arm and turn him at the same time drawing back his other fist.

"Try your game on with——"

Accepting the invitation even before it ended Dusty moved. His left fist sank almost wrist deep in Madlarn's fat belly, bringing forth a grunt of agony and making the big man stagger a couple of paces backwards. Dusty leapt in after him, the right fist ripping up to catch the offered jaw, snap Madlarn's head back and throw him backwards but not down. This was not due to lack of power but because the big man crashed into the bar and hung there with glassy eyes and mouth hanging open.

The two bardogs showed loyalty if not good sense. The one known as Kete came around the bar at the far end while his partner, Tuck, hurled clean over it and at Dusty with arms ready to grab and mangle. He hurled himself at the small Texan like a cougar at a cottontail rabbit.

Only Dusty was more dangerous than any cottontail. His danger in such a situation increased due to the teachings of a small, slit-eyed, yellow-skinned gentleman of oriental birth, who served as valet to Ole Devil Hardin. From Tommy Okasi, Japanese, not Chinese as many thought, Dusty learned the secrets of ju-jitsu and karate. These gave him an added power and advantage over bigger and stronger men as he proceeded to demonstrate.

Tuck saw Dusty going backwards even before being touched and might have put this down to the power of his personality scaring the small Texan into a swoon had he been given time to think. Before Tuck's never fast-

moving thoughts started to work on this phenomenon
he felt his shirt front gripped, two feet placed in his
stomach. He lost his balance, felt as if the world had
suddenly spun around and he was flying. Only he did
not land with the grace of a bird but rather smashed
down hard on to his back.

Taking his chance the other bardog charged forward,
lifting his foot to stomp Dusty into the woodwork as
Tuck sailed over and clear, Dusty caught the down-
driving foot, bracing himself and holding it between his
hands. Then he rolled his hips so that he hooked one leg
behind Kete's other leg, placed his other leg against the
front and heaved. With a yell Kete sprawled across the
room, hit the wall and went to his hands and knees by
the table where Mark and the Kid sat. Muttering curses
under his breath he rolled to a sitting position and
dropped his hand to the gun at his side.

"Loose it, hombre!" purred a voice mean as a
diamondback rattling a warning. "You wouldn't look
good with a mouth under your chin."

Obligingly Kete let it loose. A bowie knife-point
pricking the neck being always a fine inducement to
complaisance. He looked up into a pair of red hazel eyes
and a babyishly innocent face, although to his mind the
face was far from being either. Not for a moment did he
doubt that failure to obey would see the knife go home
into flesh. He raised no objection when the Kid lifted
the revolver from his holster but what came next was
something of a surprise.

"Now you can try your luck," said the Kid.

From before Kete's eyes came a scene which should
call for his interference or aid. Yet the quiet spoken
words worried him.

"You—you mean I can go back and help my boss
now?"

"Why sure. Don't make no never mind to me happen
you figure on tangling with Dusty again. It's your fool
hide, not mine."

The words jarred Kete down to his toes. He'd thought the Texans to be a couple of hired guns on hand to back up and keep the new officer from harm. Yet they showed a strange way of doing it as neither offered to help him, and the blackdressed one had sheathed his knife once the gun did not threaten the captain. Like Tuck, Kete did not think fast or brightly. Yet even he could add two and two to make four. The Texan knew his small *amigo* could handle the threat. So Kete decided to stay out and watch developments.

They came fast and showed his wisdom in waiting. Dusty made his feet in a rapid bound as Madlarn came from the bar. Behind Dusty, Tuck had also stood up and, bottle in hand, made for Dusty's back.

For an instant Mark thought he'd need to lend a hand. Then he saw his help would not be required, saw also that Dusty had won over the big Irishman.

With an angry yell Magoon hurled himself forward. His big fist drove out in a looping, power-packed smash which caught Tuck at the side of the jaw and knocked him clear from his feet, across the room and into the wall. Tuck lit down hard and did not look like he'd be getting to his feet for a spell.

On his part Karl Madlarn found himself learning what not a few would-be hard cases found to their cost when they tangled with Dusty Fog. He had a name as a hard-case rough-house fighter but was on the muscle with little or no science to back it. Against most people Madlarn tangled with such tactics worked for they fought in the same manner and he'd his two helpers when things got rough. Now he had no helpers for Tuck couldn't get up and Kete didn't aim to cut in, having troubles of his own. The final point against Madlarn was that Dusty did not rely on muscle.

Going under the punch, powerful enough to have put him down for hours had it landed, but slow and tele-graphed to Dusty, the small Texan again smashed Mad-larn in the middle. The big man let out a croak of agony. His hands jerked out and Dusty caught the right between his hands, pivoted so the man's stomach rested against him then, with a bending of the knees, sent him flying over with the ju-jitsu *Kata seoi*, the one-side shoulder throw which looked so spectacular and landed an unprepared man down hard. The watching soldiers gasped their amazement, for they'd never seen a wrestling throw quite like it. Nor had Madlarn, although he did not air his views on the subject for some considerable time to come.

Before the winded and dazed man had time to recover Dusty hauled him again to his feet, smashed a punch into his stomach. Madlarn's back arched once and then went limp and he lay without a move on the floor.

Turning to face Kete who still stood by the wall, Magoon asked, "The captain or me, Kete?"

Dusty threw a glance at the big man, noting the marks left when three chevrons went. He guessed Magoon's identity and guessed the sort of man he dealt with, or would soon be dealing with. Then he looked across the room at Kete, saw the gun on the table and wondered what story lay behind it.

For his part Kete wanted none of either man. He might have chanced his luck with Dusty but some nagging doubt held him back and he guessed he'd be worse than a fool if he tried conclusions with the small Texan. Kete had a reputation for being tough man, but he knew big Paddy Magoon to be tougher and nothing he'd so far seen led him to believe the small captain was any less tough than Magoon.

"Not me, Magoon," he answered. "I was only fixing to help the boss."

The Kid looked up at Kete, a mocking smile playing on his lips.

"Mister," he said. "I done wronged you considerable. I thought you hadn't the sense of a seam-squirrel, but you have."

Given the right set of circumstances Kete might have

objected to the words. However, the Kid was cold sober, armed and looked full capable of using those arms, so Kete passed up the chance. Studying the Indian dark face Kete knew that here was no boy but a man grown and a deadly dangerous man at that.

Silence fell on the room, every eye went first to Madlarn, then to the small figure in the captain's uniform. This was their new commanding officer, the man whose bugle call they ignored. Something warned every man, sobering the drunks and worrying the sober, that he would not wave it aside as something of no importance. They were going to pay for their indiscretion in sweat and hard work if nothing worse. Yet the more sober men knew that this newly arrived captain would make sure the sweat was expended on useful work, not take his anger out on them uselessly.

"This place is off limits until I reverse the order," Dusty snapped. "Now clear it, all of you!"

"Yez heard the captain, darlin's," Magoon bellowed. "Outside, every last son of ye. O'Brien, Klaus, take Dutchy with yez." He turned to Dusty and threw himself into a smart brace, with chest sticking out and arms tightly at his side, "Ye'll have to excuse Dutchy, Cap'n darlin'. 'Tis a touch of the grippe he had. It allus makes him ornery and there wasn't nothing but medicine in that bottle. We puts it in a whisky bottle to make him drink it down."

"You're Magoon, aren't you?" Dusty asked, ignoring the comments on Dutchy, other than to consider them the efforts of a sergeant trying to keep a good soldier from facing the consequences of his actions. It was also the sort of explanation a fighting soldier would make to an officer he liked and respected, one who could be expected to understand such things.

"I am, sir."

"I thought so. A brawler, a tavern-loafer. I want to see you in my office as soon as I dismiss the assembly parade that's coming."

"I thought you might, sir," replied Magoon.

"Then get back and make yourself fit to enter your commanding officer's office."

Magoon threw a salute fresh from the pages of the drill manual. He made a rapid about face and hit the door on the double, urging the others back to the fort with lusty bellows and lurid curses. His popularity and respect as both man and non-com showed in the way none of them raised any objection to his ordering them around.

Mark and the Kid walked across the room to join Dusty. He grinned at them and asked, "How the hell do we get tied in with things like this?"

"Just fortunate, I reckon," grinned the Kid. "You sure got that big mick on your side of the rope."

"Watch this bunch here, Dusty," Mark warned as they headed for the door. "The boss was sure trying to stir up those blue-bellies against you."

"I'll watch him. I'd've thought he'd make a try at getting friendly with the new post officer," drawled Dusty as they left the room. "I'll not be sorry to see the officers and sergeants learn what the situation is in camp. There's more to Mr. Madlarn's game than meets the eye. He wanted to keep the battalion disorganized and ready to bust at the seams."

They strolled back in the wake of the soldiers who were being chivvied on like a flock of chickens by a farmer's wife, although Magoon would not have cared for the simile. Such was the haste of the ex-revellers that they did not even notice an unknown sentry stood at the gates. They'd all but one idea in mind, get out of the new officer's way as quickly as possible.

In this they did not have much success for no sooner had they disappeared into their quarters than they heard the notes of assembly blown. This time none of them sat around thinking about what they should do. With one rush they headed for the parade square.

Dusty found a much more satisfactory muster of men

when he stepped from his office. Now only the third lieutenant appeared to be absent and that could be excused as he could hardly be expected to know the new commanding officer had arrived. So only Jarrow's company had an officer and sergeant before it, Gilbey stood before his and a sergeant commanded the third. Beyond the third company, among the branch personnel, stood a tall, gangling sergeant who Dusty thought looked familiar.

With cold eyes studying the ranks before him Dusty saw much that did not meet with his approval. The men were untidy, more so than just with work and old uniforms. They looked untidy through lack of supervision like troops allowed to slacken and become inefficient.

"Soldiers!" he barked. "I've seen better in a stinking Ya—border raiders' camp."

Just in time Dusty prevented himself saying Yankee border raiders' camp. He knew van Druten would never say such a thing. While wanting the officers and men to know his name, if not his correct military standing, he wanted to do it in his own way. They would not think little enough about the change in regimental plans, some of them might even believe it to be an improvement.

"Since I arrived at Fort Tucker I've seen enough to sicken me," he went on. "You're supposed to be in the U.S. cavalry and as such the defenders of this section of the Dakotas. From what I've seen since my arrival you'd need help to defend yourselves. It'll change. I want you to know, there'll be changes made. Major Lingley didn't leave you in this state and I don't intend you to stay in it. From this day the Fort sutler's store is off limits for the purchase of liquor. The town is off limits also, until such time as I decide you're fit and capable of being allowed outside the Fort."

Not a sound, not by a flicker of their faces did any of the men dare show their surprise at the words. They liked their drinking and it was the only entertainment in this lonely outpost, now they were being denied it.

"Mr. Gilbey," Dusty concluded his speech. "I want a
full inspection of the Fort tomorrow. And don't tell me
it's Sunday, I'm fully aware of that. I also want every
man paraded in review order at ten o'clock. Dismiss the
battalion."

"Yo!" Gilbey answered.

"All officers and sergeants to my office in fifteen
minutes, Mr. Gilbey, and send Private Magoon in
now."

"Yo!"

Without a backward glance Dusty returned to his office and Gilbey dismissed the parade. The mutter of the
men, discussing Dusty's orders, complaining about the
sutler's and town being places off limits, rose as the
parade broke up. The general feeling seemed to be
they'd deserved what they got and likely things would be
far different from now on. The sergeants were watching
their men and Hogan came to suggest that Gilbey held
the parade until they'd arranged working details.

One thing they all knew for sure. The full inspection
meant every building, store and animal of the Fort as
well as the men's own kit, arms and mounts. On top of
that the men knew they would find themselves with no
time to go to either the sutler's or town even if they
could, for they'd much to do to be ready for a full inspection and the review parade.

Following Hogan's advice Gilbey ordered the men to
stay on the square. He mopped his brow as he saw the
sergeants in charge of the veterinary, medical, blacksmith, quartermaster branches heading for him, all after
men to help with the cleaning and general working of
their departments. Sergeant Milt Granger ambled up
with a request for a party to help groom his reserve
horses. The young lieutenant groaned inside, while trying to avoid showing his feeling. He knew the laxness of
the past few weeks was bouncing back on his head and
he must work the men hard to putting things right.

So Gilbey began to do so. He told off working parties, sent men off to help in the various branches. The remainder felt little pleasure at not being called, for it would fall on them to prepare the barrack blocks. Gilbey snapped his orders, he gave the sergeants a brief time to organize before they would be taken to see the new commanding officer. In a few moments the parade square was bustling with men, and the center of it Gilbey stood silently cursing the absent Second-Lieutenant Cardon for not having returned to help with the work.

"Passing in two riders," called the sentry at the gate.

Wondering if some fresh devilment had come up to plague him Gilbey turned to see who the riders might be. He saw Cardon riding through accompanied by Joanna Lingley and noticed the way they both stared at the activity. With his hands behind his back, trying to look as much like Dusty Fog as he could manage, Gilbey strode forward to put Cardon to work.

CHAPTER SIX

You're Not Dandy Van Druten

In a way Dusty Fog quite looked forward to his forth-coming interview with Magoon. Since his earliest days Dusty had felt the greatest admiration for the tough hard-bitten, brave and often un-military type of ser-geant represented by the big Irishman. His kind, rarely, if ever, held their rank at boot camp in the pampered east, where drill and spit-and-polish ruled the roost. Put them out on the frontier, with wild Indians to fight and they came into their own as natural leaders. Dusty had a shrewd idea he'd remember this interview for the rest of his life for Magoon did not strike him as a respecter of rank, unless he also held in respect the man with the rank.

Standing before the desk, rigid at a brace, with his chest puffed out and stomach held in, Magoon waited, not moving a muscle. Ten seconds ticked by and Dusty gave no sign of knowing the man stood there. With somebody he disliked, or did not respect, Magoon might have coughed, or even asked a question. With Dusty he did nothing, just stayed in his brace.

"They tell me you're an insolent soldier, Magoon," Dusty finally said, looking straight at Magoon, having noticed the big man seemed to have made an effort to tidy up his appearance before reporting. "Are you only insolent within the bounds of the *Manual of Field Regulations*?"

"That I am not, Cap'n—sir," replied Magoon indignantly and sticking to the formal sir until more sure of his ground. "If I'm insolent I do it right out and I don't hide behind any book at all."

It took some doing to hold down a smile but Dusty made it. He knew Magoon respected his fighting skill and recognized another combat soldier, one who would be willing to toss aside the *Manual of Field Regulations* if he felt they impeded his duty. Dust thought fast, trying to decide just how he should give Magoon the three stripes back without endangering discipline or losing Magoon's respect.

"Would you like to be insolent with me?" he asked.

"That I wouldn't, Cap'n darlin'," answered Magoon, clearly deciding Dusty was the sort of officer he liked and who would accept the slight relaxing of discipline from an efficient man. "Sure, I'm not a smart man, but any time I wants a busted jaw I'll got to the hoss lines and let a mule do it. It'd be a lot gentler'n you. But wasn't that the elegant right hand you had down at Madlarn's. I've never——"

"You're at attention!" barked Dusty as Magoon forgot himself enough to lift his fists and start to demonstrate Dusty's technique.

Magoon slammed back into his brace once more. Slowly Dusty pushed back his chair, rose and walked around the desk, circling the man. Only by going around behind Magoon's back could Dusty prevent the man from seeing his smile. Dusty might be able to make the rest of the battalion believe he was a grim, bow-necked officer, who would brook no relaxation of discipline, but he couldn't get away with it when in Magoon's presence. Magoon could read him, tell he wanted nothing more than get the parade work over and have the men acting like a trained troop of fighting soldiers. The big Irishman stood rigid but tried to take quick glances over his shouder to see what Dusty was up to, freezing back into his brace each time he thought

Dusty's eyes rested upon him.

Before Dusty could either return to the seat behind
the desk, before he could even step from behind
Magoon he heard the door of the office thrown open.
Swinging around Dusty opened his mouth to bellow out
a demand for an explanation from whoever entered why
the hell they did so without knocking. The words died
unsaid, for Dusty would never think of employing those
sort of terms to a lady.

A lady stood just inside the office door, a young lady
but one with the undefinable air that only birth and
breeding could give. She came to a halt, her face suddenly reddening in a blush as her eyes rested on Dusty's
face. Behind her, looking very worried, stood Gilbey,
clearly he'd been trying to stop her entering the room.
Dusty studied the girl without speaking, guessing she'd
be Joanna Lingley, daughter of the late Fort Commander.

"Don't say a word, Paddy," she'd been saying as she
came in. "Don't let h—— You're not Dandy van
Druten!"

"I don't recollect I ever said I was, ma'am," Dusty
answered. "There was a last-minute change of arrangements and I came instead of Captain van Druten."

Dusty looked the girl over. Joanna Lingley was a tall
willowy girl although she'd curves in the places where a
lady might be expected to have them and the severe
riding habit she wore did not hide the curves. On her
head perched a black Stetson hat, her auburn hair
combed neatly though not fussily under it. Her face,
while not being out and out beautiful, had good looks
of an enduring kind, the sort of looks which stayed
when a more striking beauty would have felt the ravages
of time. She appeared to be somewhat confused by his
words.

"But—I—what——"

"You'd better present us, Mr. Gilbey," Dusty put in.

"Yes, sir," clearly Gilbey was puzzled as he replied.

"This is Miss Joanna Lingley, Captain——"

"Fog, ma'am," Dusty introduced. "Dustine Fog."

Joanna and Gilbey exchanged glances. "Fog?" gasped the girl. "I haven't met you, Captain Fog. I didn't know you belonged to the——"

"Fog," repeated Gilbey, also troubled, studying the way Dusty's borrowed uniform fit. "Dusti—Dusty Fog. You're Captain Dusty Fog, sir."

"Yes, mister."

"Then you took General Grant's Moshogen offer, sir."

"I'm wearing the uniform, aren't I, mister?" answered Dusty evasively but it appeared to satisfy Gilbey. "Can I help you in any way, Miss Lingley?"

The girl's face had turned scarlet and she made an effort to meet Dusty's eyes. She felt embarrassed and did not wish to air her reasons in front of the two men, even though she'd broken a strict rule to try and help one of them.

"You're dismissed, gentlemen, wait outside until I've finished."

Not until the door closed behind Magoon and Gilbey did Dusty even give a sign of knowing the girl was present. Then he drew up a chair and asked her to take a seat. Joanna sat down, studying Dusty and comparing him with the Dandy van Druten she'd known, not to the latter's advantage. All her life Joanna had lived around and among soldiers, apart for the years of school in the east, then that had mostly been in garrison towns. She knew army officers, could tell glory hunters like the Custer family, a no-good trouble causer living on family influence like van Druten. She could also tell a real genuine career officer, a man with that rare flair to be a true leader. She knew Dusty Fog to be such a man. Even in the few seconds she'd known him Joanna had read Dusty's character right. She'd seen the way Gilbey acted, the way the soldiers behaved outside and already could see the change the small Texan brought about.

"Why'd you come dashing in here like Calamity Jane to the rescue when you heard I'd called Magoon in for an interview?" he asked.

"Well, I——" the words floundered off, then Joanna stiffened slightly in her chair. Captain Fog must be fully aware of van Druten's character. "I knew Dandy van Druten both as a child and as a junior lieutenant in Washington. He'd've brought Paddy in to goad him into something more serious than insolence, so he could use Paddy as an example."

"I could have been doing the same thing."

"I know *you* wouldn't," she replied. "And do I apologize for bursting in on you like that. May I show how contrite I am by asking you to dine with me this evening?"

"It'd be my pleasure, ma'am."

"May I ask the lieutenants?"

"It's your choice, ma'am," replied Dusty with a grin. "I'd like a chance to meet them in less formal surroundings. Mr. Jarrow seems to be avoiding me and I think Mr. Cardon or whatever his name is'll be wishing he had when I see him."

Joanna chuckled, thinking of the look of horror on Gilbey's face when he heard her say she meant to go along and help out Magoon before his temper and tongue got him into worse trouble. She'd also seen enough, on returning to the Fort, to let her know Jarrow and Gilbey respected their new captain.

Knowing that she'd better not waste any more time Joanna rose to her feet and Dusty stood up, then strode to the door to open it for her. Gilbey, Magoon and the men wanting to see Dusty, stiffened into a brace as he appeared. Joanna could see Cardon looked worried and knew Jarrow had been filling him in with the details of the new captain's behavior since arrival. The girl smiled and passed along the porch of the building for she heard what Dusty said.

"Sergeant Magoon, you're out of uniform. I'll excuse

it this once. Get your chevrons stitched on as soon as
you're finished here then take over as sergeant of the
guard—for a week.''

The look on Magoon's face made Dusty's day complete. The big Irishman stood at a brace and a whole
gamut of emotions ran over his face, delight, surprise,
relief, then the realization of what Dusty's last words
meant. Dusty heard the girl chuckle and knew she had
not missed the point of the punishment. With Gilbey officer of the day for a week, he would be thrown almost
twenty-four hours a day in contact with Magoon. If
they could get along through that period they would
manage for the rest of their time together.

''I might add, Sergeant Magoon, that it's by Mr.
Gibley's recommendation I've struck the court martial
from your record,'' Dusty went on. ''Bring the gentlemen in, Mr. Gilbey.''

Sitting at his desk Dusty watched the officers, sergeants and scouts come to a halt in a group before him.
For a moment his eyes rested on Sergeant Kallan but the
man's face gave no sign of his thoughts. Yet he looked
puzzled and might at any time start to raise some point
which Dusty would be unable to talk away. So Dusty
did not give him the chance.

''Introduce the gentlemen, Mr. Gilbey,'' he said.

Quickly Gilbey introduced the officers. Dusty gave
Cardon a cold look which made the young officer consider his past sins. Then Gilbey went on to present the
sergeants. Studying the non-coms Dusty decided they
were all competent, reliable men who only needed
shaking together and reminding of their duties. With
men like them behind him he would find little difficulty
in throwing the Fort into shape once more. There were
the three company sergeants now Magoon was rein-
stated and the branch sergeants who attended to the
maintenance and welfare of the fort. These latter would
require tactful handling for they were the heads of their
department and as such would want their own problems

regarded as of being vitally important.

"We'll most likely get to know each other better, gentlemen," said Dusty at the end. "I don't doubt Mr. Gilbey warned you that, due to a change of orders, I've taken command instead of Captain van Druten."

From the look of the men's faces Gilbey had not mentioned it, a point in his favor Dusty conceded. The men all looked interested, specially Kallan who served as drill instructor and would have been at West Point about the time a man Dusty's age joined it. Dusty guessed what the man thought and went on:

"My name is Fog, Dusty Fog."

It is said much for the discipline of the men that they did not show their surprise at his words. Yet he could tell every one of the men, with the exception of Mark and the Kid, were interested in his words. He could also tell that not one of them thought anything other than he'd accepted the offer made by General Grant at the Moshogen court house during the war.

"Now, gentlemen, let's get down to deciding how we can bring the Fort and battalion back to efficient standards."

After arranging for the tightening of discipline, Dusty asked for a map of their patrol area. Dismissing the non-operational men, he asked about the Indian situation.

"I tell you Cap'n," said a leathery, white-haired old scout known as Sucataw Joe, showing more respect and politeness than Gilbey could remember since Major Lingley died. "Old Eagle Catcher's getting a mite riled."

"More'n a mite," grunted another scout, known as Rowdy because he spoke very little. "Effen we can't stop them rushers getting in there'll be all hell to pay on this side of the Belle Pourche."

"Which same we're here to prevent," Dusty replied. "You may have heard we ran into a bunch of Hunkpapa Sioux on the way here."

"Likely some of Crazy Bear's lodge brothers," drawled Sucataw. "They'll be back over the Belle Pourche now and talking war talk some, even though they got licked. That'd slow the war talk some, but them rushers getting in'll keep the fire fanned until Crazy Bear can get up strong enough medicine to bring the rest out."

"Which same we're going to prevent," Dusty told the others. "How've you been handling the situation, Mr. Gilbey?"

"I've had a patrol out, sir. Changed its direction regularly, but there's a lot of range to cover and the rushers seem to be able to anticipate our moves so a steady trickle gets in."

"The lootenant did think as how these rushers might be getting to know which way he was going, Cap'n,' put in Magoon. "Which same was the cause of our little disagreement."

"Explain that, mister," said Dusty.

Gilbey stiffened slightly. It had not been his idea, but Magoon's, that somehow or other the rushers learned which way the patrol might be going. He also remembered the big sergeant laid the blame for the information leaks on Madlarn.

"The patrols always knew where they would be going the day before, sir. It allowed them to make arrangements for what supplies and gear to take along. Sergeant Magoon thought that the members of the patrol might be talking to somebody outside the Fort and they used their knowledge to help the rushers."

"You took no precautions against their hearing?"

"I tried, sir, but the rushers still appeared to find out."

Studying the map, Dusty asked questions about the lie of the land with especial interest in the course of the Belle Pourche River.

"There look to be four places at most where rushers can get over fast and easy," Dusty finally said and the men who knew the river nodded their heads. "Which same'll be the most likely places for them to make for."

"You called it right, Cap'n," grunted Sucataw.

"But they are too far apart for us to be able to cover adequately with the men at our disposal," Dusty went on. "We need a garrison of at least one company for the Fort. So we'll have a patrol of thirty men out at all times, under the command of one officer and sergeant. It's not going to be easy, gentlemen, on any of you. The direction of the patrol will be my decision. I'll hand it to the patrol commander in a sealed envelope which he will not open until at least a mile past Shacktown and sure he is not being followed. The patrol will split into two parts, officer taking fifteen men, sergeant taking fifteen and you'll work the areas I've put in your orders."

From that point Dusty went on to tell the men how they would make the patrols. Much to his concern, Cardon learned that he would be taking out the first party within thirty minutes of the review parade's completion. To ensure complete coverage of their patrol area would not be easy; the leisurely days at Fort Tucker had come to an end.

"It'll be rough on the men, sir," Gilbert remarked.

"They're paid for it, mister," Dusty replied. "And it'll be a damned sight rougher if the Sioux junp the Belle Pourche."

Much as Dusty wished to ride out and study the ground, he knew he could not for some days to come. Not only must he stay in the Fort and continue to make his presence felt, but he would also be involved in the routine of assuming formal command. Not to do so would arouse suspicion. Fortunately the Confederate Army had modelled itself on the Yankee forces, so Dusty knew what he must do when taking over.

"Thank you, gentlemen," he said when the last details had been arranged. "I won't keep you from your work any longer. Mr. Gilbey, Miss Lingley has invited the officers to dine with her. We'll all attend, you are permitted to come for dinner, although I don't expect it to interfere with your duties. I warn you all, no word of the patrol must be allowed to get out. You will tell nobody, your wives, your company, not even your strikers. I don't want anyone to know of the patrol until after the review. Dismissed, gentlemen.''

The men saluted and filed from the room. Hogan and the two Texans remained and after the door closed Mark grinned broadly.

"You sure started something," he said, "I near on jumped through the roof when you told them your right name."

Dusty shrugged. "I had to do it, there's too many folks here knew van Druten so I had to let on who I was and rely on folks thinking I'd joined the Yankee army after all."

"Reckon I'll go and jaw a spell with Sucataw and the other scouts, " drawled the Kid. "I'll lend a hand with the scouting as soon as I know the country. Unless the captain's got other ideas for me."

"None at all, be a change to see you working," grunted Dusty. "You stay on and lend a hand, Mark, ride with Lon on scout. I reckon every bit of help'll be needed once we start moving. I'm going to my quarters now, Sergeant-major. Keep the men at it."

Throughout the Fort men scrubbed, scraped, painted, removed dirt and debris to burn outside the Fort. They worked hard, being driven on by the non-coms and supervised by the officers. Until darkness fell horses were still being groomed in the lines and everywhere sweating, cursing men made sure nothing would offend their new captain's eyes in the morning.

Even when the main cleaning-up work was done the men had not finished. In the barrack blocks and houses soldiers now set to work to clean up their gear and make sure they'd look at their best in the morning. Not one of them chanced breaking Dusty's rule that the town and sutler's store were out of bounds. They would not have had the time, nor would they been able to get through any of the gates even if they'd wished to go drinking.

In the room which Dusty took as his quarters he found his striker waiting for him. The old soldier had been Major Lingley's striker and knew how to handle an officer's belongings. He appeared to work as much for Joanna as for Dusty and warned that dinner would be served at eight o'clock, then went to fetch hot water for Dusty to wash and shave. Finally he took van Druten's keys from Dusty, opened the late captain's box and got out the dress uniform.

Dusty had not found time to unpack any of his personal belongings, but they were in the room where Mark and the Kid stayed. He went along to collect his razor and shaving gear from his warbag but left the rest of his belongings where they were until he could bring them in without the striker seeing them.

"Perhaps you'd like to go and see Miss Joanna before the other gentlemen arrive, sir?" said Dawkins, the striker. He'd been a butler but followed his master into the Union army, saw him killed and became striker for Major Lingley, then a full colonel. Like so many officers, Lingley lost rank when war ended. Dawkins, however, he never lost and the old man did much to make life comfortable for his officer.

"Be a good idea," Dusty agreed, allowing Dawkins to help him into van Druten's dress coat. Dusty was now washed, shaved and wearing the best uniform, with his sword belt at his side. He left the officers' quarters and headed for the Lingley house, knocking on the door. An old Negress opened it, a woman who'd been with the Lingley family ever since Lingley married the daughter of a southern plantation owner and he presented the couple with her as a servant.

Allowing Dusty to enter the old woman took his hat and escorted him along a passage to the sitting-room. Joanna rose from the table to greet Dusty but did not come towards him. There were several newspapers on the table, one of which Dusty would have preferred not to see.

The door closed behind him and Joanna's hand dropped, going under the newspaper to lift out a Colt Baby Dragoon revolver. She lined it at him, cocking the hammer in a way which showed she knew how to use it.

"Stand right there, Captain Fog, for that's your real name."

"*The Bismark Herald*," Dusty drawled with a smile. "I should have thought of that. We brought the mail and likely some newspapers in."

"That's right, you should. There's an interesting item on the front page. About a trailherd brought in by the Texas gunfighter and rancher, Dusty Fog. You deny it of course?"

"Yes ma'am. I'm neither a gunfighter or a rancher. I've had to use my guns more'n a little, but I never laid claim to being a gunfighter. And I'm segundo of the OD Connected, not a rancher. I've got the money for the herd and enough to identify me in my warbag."

The gun barrel lowered a trifle. "But you couldn't have enlisted——"

"I didn't, officially."

Joanna brought the gun into line once more. Dusty walked forward slowly, ignoring it completely. The girl's face showed her sudden worry but she did not try to squeeze the trigger.

"You better explain," she suggested.

Quickly Dusty explained, told of the reasons he'd come to the Fort. He saw the revolver muzzle lower until it pointed towards the table top. The girl lowered the Colt's hammer on to a safety notch and laid it aside. She smiled and relaxed.

"I see," she said, and meant it. "But we'd better keep the paper from out of Frank and the boys' hands. You're right of course and I don't think I know of another civilian in the country who could have done what you've done today."

"Shucks, you'll be making me blush next," Dusty grinned.

"I arranged for the ladies of the Fort to come and meet you after dinner," she went on. "I suppose I ought to have waited for permission but—"

"I'd like you to carry on arranging things like that for me until you leave, or I do," Dusty replied. "If you wish to leave earlier than when the wagons go back in a month I'll try and arrange it."

"I'll wait. I might even be able to help you when the new relief arrives," she replied, then began to chuckle as she hid the papers and her revolver. "You've made quite an impression since your arrival. I've already heard four versions of how you whipped Madlarn and his men, all most complimentary to you."

"Reckon anybody suspects I'm not an officer, apart from you?"

"I doubt it," she smiled and cocked her head as a knock sounded at the ouside door. "And I wouldn't want to be the person to try to convince your men you aren't what you seem. Shall we go in to meet our guests, Captain Fog?"

CHAPTER SEVEN

Noreen's Indiscretions

Like most of the Fort's occupants, Noreen Kallan attended the review parade and watched the patrol ride out. She noticed the difference in the bearing and appearance of the men and knew that few had managed to grab more than a couple of hours' sleep the previous night. However, Captain Fog seemed to be satisfied. After watching the patrol's departure, Noreen left the Fort's confines and made for the rear of the postsutler's building. Opening the door, she walked into Madlarn's living quarters.

Tuck, his jaw swollen, opened the door for her, did not trouble to ask any questions but allowed her to enter. Clearly Noreen knew where she was going for she went to a door at the side of the passage, opened it and walked in.

Stripped to his long-john underwear Madlarn stood before the mirror trying to shave himself without touching his battered and pain-filled face. Neither he nor Noreen showed the slightest embarrassment at his lack of clothes and she leaned by the door, closing it, watching as he finished shaving and rinsed his face.

"It looks like you ran into trouble, Karl," she remarked, then came nearer. "My, he really worked you over."

Madlarn turned, his face flushing with anger and his hand drawing back. The woman showed niether fear nor worry at this but stood facing him, a taunting smile on her face. He threw the razor to one side and grabbed her, dragging her up to him and kissing her hard. Noreen kissed back, her fingernails digging into his back as she clung to him. They sank to the bed and he pressed her against it. For a long time they stayed locked in each other's arms, then he released her.

"Why'd you come here like this?" he asked. "In plain daylight."

Noreen chuckled, seeing the worried look he threw at the door. Madlarn might have charm, he might and frequently did, supply the extra loving she craved for, but she knew him for what he was. If Slasher Kallan ever found out about her and Madlarn the sutler would run or die and she guessed Madlarn would run.

"It's all right," she said, looking up at the man's battered face. "Nobody saw me, Slasher's with the other non-coms at a conference with Captain Fog."

"Fog? I thought he was Dandy van Druten."

"So did I," purred Noreen. "I went to see him just after he arrived. Thought I'd renew an old acquaintance. Only it was Dusty Fog, not Dandy when I arrived."

"Dusty Fog, that Texas gunfighter?" croaked Madlarn.

"Sure," she answered taking scarcely hidden pleasure at the fear in the man's eyes. "He was promised a commission in the army through something he did in the war. Slasher and some of the other sergeants were at our place discussing it last night. You'd think he was a kind of god the way the folks in the Fort are going on about him." She paused and sighed. "Mind you, he's all man and what a man."

Angrily Madlarn drew her up from the bed and locked his arms around her. Once more she kissed back but suddenly twisted her head from his and whispered into his ear.

"He's sent a patrol out, Karl."

Madlarn let out an angry snarl and thrust the woman from him, coming to his feet.

"He's done *what*?"

"Sent out a patrol. Thirty men under Cardon and his sergeant."

"Why in hell didn't you let me know sooner?" he snapped. "Which way're they going?"

Slowly Noreen came to her feet and looked the man over from head to foot. "I didn't know until after the parade this morning, nor did they. And they're riding under sealed orders, from what I could tell. Them and every other patrol which goes out and from what I've seen of Captain Fog that's going to be a tolerable few. No more telling which way they're headed, Karl, so you can sell the information to the rushers."

For a moment Noreen thought she'd gone too far. Malarn's face went almost black with rage and his hands clenched into fists. She faced him with her own hands clenched and such a look in her eyes that he fell back a step or two, further proving to her that she'd picked a coward to play with.

"All right, Noreen," he said. "You did your best. We'll just have to hope the bunch we sent out this morning don't get caught."

"And if they do?"

"They can't prove a thing," he answered. "They can't bring anything back to me. I've been passing the information through Bruno Lewis down at the Shacktown Saloon. I'll send Tuck to warn Bruno, he's got some tough boys on hand to help him in cases like this."

"What're you fixing to do now?" Noreen inquired.

There she had Madlarn. He did not know how he might get information from the Fort. She'd brought him much, in return for sexual pleasure. He'd learned more from the soldiers when they came to the store to drink. Now both sources of information appeared to be closed, for the man would not know where they patrolled and so the rushers could not be sent through as they used to be.

"Just how deep in are you?" Noreen asked.

"Deep enough. We've been taking money from the rushers, letting a few slip in at a time. Never enough to start the Sioux on the warpath but enough to bring a steady return for our effort."

"Who's we?"

"You know who we is. I work in with Bruno Lewis."

Noreen smiled mockingly. She knew Bruno Lewis, the head of Shacktown, the man behind the entire collection of graft and crookedness which made up the gathering point of the rushers in this area. Lewis did not have partners, only underlings and Madlarn was no more than that.

"Go send Tuck to tell him," she said.

While Madlarn was gone Noreen stripped off her clothes and on his return she lay on the bed. Her eyes mocked him as she looked up towards him.

"All this time you've been using me, Karl honey. Now I'm the only one between you and the rushers. I'm the only one who might find out where the patrols will be hiding. You're going to pay for every bit of information, Karl—and you're going to pay in advance."

Madlarn sank on to the bed by the woman. He knew what she said to be true. If anyone in the Fort might possibly learn where the patrols went it would be Noreen and he would have to pay her the way she wanted. No longer could he wave her aside when he did not feel like love-making. No longer would she beg him to come into his room and satisfy her lust. Now it would be different, she held the reins, the whip, and could set the spurs any time she wished.

In the Fort the tightening-up process began, or continued at full pace. The results were showing already. Word reached Dusty, via a rider sent back from Cardon's patrol, that five different groups of rushers had been spotted and turned back from the Belle Pourche River. Dusty knew his plan was working, he also knew that whoever let the rushers know they would slip through was going to need some smart explaining when these parties returned.

He did not know that an exhausted Madlarn received a visit from Bruno Lewis late that night, an angry man demanding to know why he'd been given wrong information about the patrols.

"I've got ten men down there," Lewis snarled. "They want their money back, or word of how to get in."

Madlarn studied his boss. Lewis was not a tall man, his face had the sallow color of old parchment and his dark eyes were colder than any snake's. He wore a sober black suit and hat, a cheap white shirt and bow tie. Yet he ran Shacktown and controlled the crooked bunch who stayed there and rooked the rushers. He did it by brains and organizing ability, for he never wore a gun. Yet he was feared in the town, for when he pointed his finger a man died. Backing Lewis were a trio of dangerous killers, he did not need to wear a gun.

"There's a new boss at the Fort," Madlarn finally replied. "He's playing it smart. Closed down my place and set your town off limits."

"Dandy van Druten did that?" snarled Lewis. "I'd better go and see him."

"It won't do any good. That's not Dandy van Druten at the Fort."

"Who is it then?"

"Dusty Fog. That Texas gunfighter. He's joined the army and they sent him out instead of van Druten."

The words had their effect on Lewis. He managed to hold down the expression which came to his face, but failed in it for he knew all too well who Dusty Fog was. Lewis knew van Druten, had some information the young captain would not wish to be made public. Yet it would do him no good at all now for van Druten did not command the Fort.

"I thought you told me you'd got the Fort tied up," Lewis said quietly. "The men ready to mutiny and pull out."

"I was well on the way to it when he arrived. But he's got them back again. He came here yesterday and worked me over—him and that dammed dumb mick, Magoon."

"Then you'll have to do what you can," Lewis warned. "I've got men waiting to go over the river and they want to get over without being caught or sent back. Don't you see what sort of a position you put me in. I get the rushers into the Black Hills, they take the chances, dig the gold and we get most of it from them when they come out. I'm not standing back and letting any damn gunfighter scare me off or cost me money."

"I'll do what I can, boss," answered Madlarn sullenly.

"How about that gal, that sergeant's wife, Noreen?"

Madlarn could have groaned at the thought of her. His body ached from her clawing hands and biting teeth. She'd only just left before Lewis arrived and the sutler still felt the effects of her love-making.

"She'll do what she can."

"All right, see she does and keep her happy," Lewis ordered. "I've an idea she's the only one who might be able to help us."

With that Lewis left the room and Madlarn sank to his bed groaning and holding his head. Things were getting to the stage where he felt he'd best pull out and head east to a healthier climate. Only he'd have to go careful or he'd be likely to wind up with a bullet in his head, for Lewis had not paid out good money to put him into the sutler's store and then allow him to run out when the going got a bit rough.

Unaware, although suspecting his plans might be making life awkward for folks, Dusty carried on with his plans for making the Fort efficient once more. He began the tricky task of building up the morale of the men. First he had to jolt them out of their complacency, revive their pride in being cavalrymen. This called for skilled judgement, for knowledge of men. It was a time for instant obedience of orders, of discipline enforced to the letter, a time when punishment awarded must be exactly right, neither too much nor too little.

For a regular career officer, his future at stake as an inducement, it would have been a difficult enough time. For Dusty it was even more so as he had no such inducements. He was here to do an unpleasant job forced on to him by circumstances and he aimed to do it well. So he seemed to be everywhere, and wherever he went he expected work to be done well. He praised, he cursed, he awarded field punishment, pack drill, extra work but always so fairly that the men who received the punishment admitted they got no more than they deserved.

The patrols came and went. They would come in secret and go in secret. No man could say for sure how many patrols were out or how they would be divided. The rushers never knew when they might be able to slip across the Belle Pourche and seek for the pot of gold at the end of the Custer-inspired rainbow. Many tried but each time a patrol arrived in time to catch them and turn them back. In the first week not one rusher managed to cross the river.

To the men on the patrols it meant long hours in the saddle and longer hours walking and leading the horses. Scouts fanned out, from high points studying the surrounding country, though they formed a chain across the area, with so few men there were blind spots, but in the first week the rushers found none.

In the Fort things were no easier for the men not on patrol. They were led by a man who did not believe in letting them grow bored by inactivity and kept every daylight hour fully occupied. There was drill, with Slasher Kallan in his glory as he put the men through their paces. Inspection, weapon training, physical training, horsemanship, stable policing, they all were used to keep the men occupied and in the first week became once more part of the lives of the soldiers.

Nor was it just in working hours Dusty kept his men going. He knew boredom could drive the men to drinking outside the Fort and so made sure nobody found time to be bored. Every company vied with the others to find the best horseman, shot, sabre fender, best drill group. Not only on military matters did they compete among themselves. The wives organized a cooking contest to be judged on the night they held their dance in the empty store cabin. A group of Scottish-born soldiers announced that Company "B" had a man who could do a sword dance better than any other soldier in the Fort and the Scots of the other companies set out to disprove it.

At the end of the first week Dusty lifted his off limits order, but few were the men who took advantage of it. The new recruits paid a visit to Shacktown but found it offered little to them. For the most part the soldiers found enough in the Fort to keep them going.

On the Monday of the second week Dusty shed his official sword belt and came on morning inspection with his own gunbelt, and matched bone-handled Colts. The easing off could begin slowly now the men did not need a constant watch being kept on them.

Just after morning muster parade Dusty strolled along through the Fort with his usual escort of Dunbrowski, Kallan and Hogan. The drill instructor, as always, wanted more time to work the soldiers. He hoped to take back at least one company as a trained drill team and that took work. Dusty used his tact to restrain Kallan for others wished to have their own departments worked.

They approached the main gates and saw that Dusty's orders for the sentry were being enforced to the letter.

In his buggy, with Cato, a tall gaunt, buckskin-dressed halfbreed at his side, Bruno Lewis looked down at the sentry. He'd rolled up to the Fort in the buggy but was halted on the outside by a grim-eyed soldier nursing a Springfield carbine across his arm.

"Come to see the captain," Lewis said, as if that would make things all right for him to enter.

"Hold it there," replied the sentry. "I'll get the sergeant of the guard."

"We ain't got time to waste with all that fooling," Cato snarled. He'd a name as a real bad man to cross and wore a low-tied Army Colt at his right side, a knife at the left. "We're going right in."

The sentry made no attempt to move, but he drew back the hammer of his carbine with a thumb and grinned bleakly.

"Don't try it, mister. You might scare me to death."

This was the first sign Bruno Lewis got that things were far different than in his last visit to the Fort. He'd been allowed in to see Gilbey without any fuss and had learned enough to enable him to slip rushers over the line for a week. He hoped to feel out the new commanding officer, to try and learn something if he could, for the rushers were getting restless. In the back of his buggy sat a thin, myopic-looking man in old clothes, one of the many drawn from the east by dreams of easy money. This man had returned from an unsuccessful attempt to cross the river and had a grievance he wished aired with Captain Fog.

"Pass the party in, sentry," Dusty called, on Kallan whispering who the gaunt man in the buggy was.

Dusty had not yet found time to go to Shacktown, although Mark and the Kid had been and brought back a report of it. However, the small Texan hoped he would get a chance to meet Bruno Lewis, who Magoon, among others, claimed was a real bad one and the power in the town.

"I'm here on a serious matter, Captain," Lewis said, climbing stiffly from the buggy and looking Dusty over, wondering if the small man could really be the famous Dusty Fog. "Your sentry didn't allow me to enter."

"On my orders, mister," Dusty replied. "You only

needed to wait until he called the sergeant of the guard and he'd have passed you in.''

Looking around him with some wonder Lewis studied the bearing and aspect of the men. For a post supposedly falling apart at the seams, Fort Tucker looked remarkably smart and well cared for. Madlarn's stories of drunkenness and idleness wearing down the men had either been grossly exaggerated or this new officer must have something which did not immediately show.

"I'm mayor of Shacktown, Captain Fog," Lewis went on. "As well as serving as local judge. This man came to me with a serious complaint."

Climbing down the rusher looked around him in wonder as if he'd never seen the inside of a fort before. He wore old clothes and his boots looked to be considerably battered. From the way he walked his feet hurt him, for he stepped like a man crossing egg shells.

"Why bother me with his complaint?" asked Dusty.

"Because he was set upon by an officer of your command. Illtreated. I am here to support his demand that disciplinary action be taken against the officer in question."

"I'd need to know more before I'll take any action."

"I've friends in Washington, and at Yankton——!" Lewis began, a threat which often worked with career officers.

"Mister, I've friends in a lot of places but I don't boast about them. Who might you be complaining about?"

"One of your lieutenants. This man was peacefully travelling when the officer stopped him, took his horse and made him walk back to Shacktown."

"From the Belle Pourche?" asked Dusty. "Sergeant Kallan, have the bugler blow for Mr. Cardon.

"From the Belle Pourche," agreed Lewis, throwing an angry look at Cato who snarled something under his breath. "Where he was merely looking——"

"I've read Mr. Cardon's report on the incident. The

man was on the Black Hills side of the river and one of
the scouts fetched him back. It had been the second time
Mr. Cardon caught him trying to cross the river.''

Lewis had come to the Fort to test the mettle of the
man in charge. He found himself tangling with a tough,
determined young officer who did not appear to fear
threats of repercussions from friends in high places.
He'd brought the rusher along to show the man how
much influence he had, only it did not seem such a good
idea now as he didn't appear to have any influence.

"That's him!" yelped the rusher, pointing to where
Cardon came running towards them in answer to the
bugle call. Then the man pointed to where Mark
Counter and the Ysabel Kid came along at a slower
pace, having been with Cardon both on the patrol in
question and when the bugle call sounded. "Them two
was the scouts with him. That black-dressed 'un came
after me across——''

The words died unsaid as Lewis thrust an elbow into
the man's ribs but it was too late. Dusty looked at the
man, then turned to Cardon who halted and brought off
a salute straight from the drill manual.

"Did you make this civilian walk from the Belle
Pourche, mister? Dusty asked, returning the salute.

"Yes, sir. As I put in my report this was the second
time I'd warned him about trying to get into the Black
Hills. I thought a stiffer lesson might work this time.''

"They made me walk while they rode around me,
Captain,'' wailed the rusher, raising one boot to show a
hole in the sole. "They made me walk back in these
boots.''

"Is that correct, mister?''

"Yes, sir,'' replied Cardon.

"You shouldn't've done it.''

Cardon's face showed it's surprise at the words. He
stared at Dusty as if he couldn't believe his ears. Since
getting to know Dusty he'd grown to expect backing
from the small Texan, yet Dusty seemed to be deserting

him in a most public manner. The rusher beamed in delight as he thought of getting his revenge on the young lieutenant. Lewis also looked pleased, he put Dusty's words down to a change of stand in the face of his threats. The small Texan must have reconsidered his words and decided to get out from under while he could. None of the officers or sergeants would follow his orders now.

"No, sir," Dusty went on. "You shouldn't have made him walk back in those boots, mister. You should have taken them off and made him do it barefoot. The next rusher you catch on his second try at crossing do just that and haul him here to the guardhouse when you get back. You acted right, mister."

Three startled faces stared at Dusty. The rusher's mouth dropped open and he seemed to be contemplating flight. Cardon's face fought to remain emotionless but he could hardly hold down a smile of delight. Lewis stood with a scowl on his face and rage filling him.

"You've no right to do that, Captain Fog," he said quietly. "I'm registering an official protest against the attitude you're encouraging among your men. I feel that as mayor of Shacktown I should be informed where your patrols will be, so as to be able to tell folks the areas to avoid."

"Yeah, I bet you would," grinned Dusty. "My patrols will be out daily and covering the length of the Belle Pourche. They've orders to turn back any rusher who tries to cross the river. I'll back them no matter how they carry out their orders. Understand that, Mr. Lewis."

"I protest it!" Lewis bellowed back. "Both as a civic leader, a citizen of the United States and a member of the bar. I'll have your coat off your back for this, Captain Fog. I'll break you——"

"If you're not out of these gates *pronto*, mister," Dusty suddenly snapped, "I'll have you thrown in the guardhouse."

"You and who else?" snarled Cato with mistimed loyalty.

"Just me," Dusty replied. "And take your hand away from your gun."

Cato stood up on the seat of the buggy, his face mean as a starving silver-tip grizzly and his hand hovering the butt of his Colt. Then suddenly the small Texan was no longer small. He stood towering above all of them, he dominated the scene.

"Sit down, Cato!" Lewis ordered. His concern was less for the possibility of shooting than for the certainty that his man would die if he tried to touch a gun.

For once Cato needed no second telling. He'd seen good men with their guns before and knew that here stood a man the equal of the best. His chances against such a man were less than nil. Slowly he sank down to the seat and reached for the reins. His boss climbed into the buggy and the rusher came towards it but Lewis snarled an order and Cato drove off without the man.

Dusty stood watching the buggy leave and the rusher hobbling painfully after it. He smiled and the smile was mirrored on the faces of the men around him.

"So endeth the first lesson," he drawled. "Let's have some work done, Mr. Cardon. And don't forget what I told you."

"No, sir," answered Cardon. "I never do, sir."

With that he headed back to supervise his company as they groomed their horses. Dusty turned to Kallan and resumed his talking as if nothing had happened but he knew it had. Lewis would have things to think about now.

CHAPTER EIGHT

Dusty's Ultimatum

Three days went by after Bruno Lewis tried, and failed, to make his impression on Dusty Fog. The rushers no longer tried to cross the Belle Pourche in daytime for fear of being caught. The few who thought of trying at night mostly gave it up for only at certain points could a night crossing be chanced and there was rarely time to make a careful study of the lie of the land without the added risk of a patrol detecting them.

In Shacktown much changed. The few rushers who remained had little money to throw around in the saloon or brothel. Bruno Lewis and his guns faced one group of indignant men but were forced to pay back money advanced for word of how to cross the Belle Pourche in safety. Lewis, in a cold rage, headed for the sutler's and warned Madlarn to either learn where the patrols went —or else.

The threat left Madlarn in a real muck-sweat, for he knew Lewis did not warn without meaning to carry it out. Madlarn's faith in himself had been severely shaken since his beating at the hands of the small Texan. His trust in the ability of Tuck and Kete had likewise undergone a reverse. He doubted if they would be capable of handling Bruno Lewis' gunmen in the event of trouble.

So Madlarn laid his cards flat before Noreen when she came in for a morning session of love-making. He did his part and then, lying beside her on the bed, looked down and tried to put on his best charm.

"You've got to find out where the patrols are, Noreen," he said.

Flat on her back, hair dishevelled and mouth hanging open a little as she caught her breath once more, Noreen Kallan looked the man over in disgust. She sat up the better to study his fattening frame and suddenly felt sickened by him. He had none of the vitality of her husband and made a poor substitute. At best Madlarn gave no more than the mechanics of live and she was finding it hard to make her imagination do the rest. Suddenly she wanted no more to do with him and felt that she must get him done with for keeps.

"How could I find out?" she asked. "The patrols go out under sealed orders. The only man who knows where they're going in advance is Captain Fog."

"Couldn't you get around him?"

The disgust and loathing showed plain in her eyes now. "I couldn't and I don't think I'd try even if I could."

"Why not?" said Madlarn in something nearer a whine than a snarl.

"You wouldn't understand, Karl. I'm not even sure I do myself. Go fetch a bottle in, will you. We'll see what we can work out."

Madlarn rose, pulled on his shirt and trousers, then headed for the bar. He wanted a drink badly and felt that after a couple of snorts of whisky and some of his charm she would agree to help. Only with Noreen's aid might he learn what he must know. Then he could kiss her goodbye for her demands proved too wearing for him. Whatever he did he must not let her know that.

In the bar Tuck and Kete were working, idly cleaning glasses. They both threw broad grins at their boss as he entered. Madlarn did not wear his coat or a tie and his shirt neck hung open, on the side of his throat, clearly visible, was a brownish oval bruise.

"Been busy, boss?" grinned Tuck.

"Shut your mouth!" snarled Madlarn, taking up a

bottle of his best whisky. "I don't need your wit."

The main doors of the building opened even as he spoke. Madlarn's face lost what little color it possessed as he saw the three men who entered.

The day was warm and Dusty Fog strolled back from watching a section of men learning sabre-fighting from horseback. With Dusty walked sergeants Magoon and Kallan, for it had been men from Magoon's company on the training and Kallan was a first-rate sabre fighter.

From his arrival Dusty had found but little time to spend with Mark and the Kid, for he was fully occupied with the running of the Fort. His two friends knew this and performed their duties as scouts for the various patrols, or spent their leisure time escorting Joanna on fishing and shooting trips, much to the annoyance of Jarrow and Cardon, who found themselves too busy to play escort.

Dusty himself saw the girl often, but he could not spend time during parade hours to be social or act as escort. This day had been a good example for he'd not found time even to return to his office since inspecting the battalion on muster parade.

"I reckon a cold beer'd go down right now," he remarked to the two sergeants. "What do you say?"

"I've never been known to refuse a beer, Cap'n darlin'," replied Magoon.

"You sure haven't," grinned Kallan. "What's Madlarn's stock like?"

"Real good and cold as a mountain stream," said Magoon, licking his lips at the prospect.

"Let's give it a whirl then," drawled Dusty, grateful that he could talk naturally instead of sticking to the way van Druten would address his men. "But if the beer's not cold you'll be sergeant of the guard every day you come off patrol."

Saying that Dusty led the way to the sutler's building. They stepped on to the porch and Kallan opened the door for Dusty, allowing him to be first to enter. Magoon went next and Kallan brought up the rear. At this hour of the morning the barroom had no customers, only the three men behind the bar.

This was the first time Dusty had entered the sutler's bar since his hectic first day. For all that he was surprised at the startled expressions he saw on the faces of Madlarn and his two men. They all stared towards him as seeing a ghost and Madlarn threw a nervous look at the door which led to his quarters and the rear of the building. Then Madlarn stood staring like a mesmerized rabbit faced by a weasel as the men came nearer.

"Three beers, Madlarn," boomed Magoon. "And make them cold, for my sake."

A look of relief came to the faces of Tuck and Kete, even Madlarn got some of the color back to his face. He nodded to Tuck who produced the bottles of beer from beneath the counter while Kete fetched out beer schooners. Madlarn ran a tongue-tip across his lips and threw another look over his shoulder towards the door.

"We don't often see you in here, Captain Fog," he said.

Whatever Dusty might have replied to the words never did get said. The door behind the bar opened and Madlarn staggered back, his hand going to the open neck of his shirt, trying to hide the bite mark on his throat. He saw the rage in Slasher Kallan's face and fell back a pace.

Dressed in her gingham frock, but fastening it up as she came through the door, without her shoes or stockings and with hair rumpled, Noreen Kallan came into the bar. The way the door opened she could not see the three customers at first and she asked:

"Where's the drink you promised me, K——"

Her voice died away as she saw her husband and the other two men beyond the bar. Her face lost its color and she stood rooted to the spot for the moment. There could be no doubt as to why she'd been in the back with Madlarn, her unbuttoned frock and lack of shoes and stockings pointed clearly to her previous actions as did the way she looked generally. She staggered slightly, her hand catching the edge of the door for support. Never had Slasher caught her out in one of her indiscretions, not until this moment.

A low, almost beastlike snarl came from Kallan's lips. He seemed to be the first one to recover from the shock of finding Noreen in the building. The woman saw her husband throw himself towards the bar, hands reaching out towards Madlarn, who backed hurriedly so his shoulders hit the wall. Noreen gave a cry of mortification and retreated through the door, slamming it behind her. She fled along the passage, pausing only to grab up her shoes, then she let herself out of the back door and fled towards the Fort. Behind her she could hear nothing and did not know what might be happening in the sutler's building, only that whatever it was her life as Slasher Kallan's wife was over.

Dusty came out of his shock at seeing Kallan's wife. He saw the sergeant leap at Madlarn and knew he must intervene or see murder done. There was no time to give orders, even if they would be obeyed. Kallan's temper had snapped and he would be deaf to any words.

So Dusty did not waste words. He struck with the *tegatana*, the handsword of karate. He did not use a clenched fist for that would be too slow to stop Kallan at such a moment. With fingers extended instead of bent, held rigidly together, thumb bent over the palm of his hand, Dusty struck as if he was making a back-hand slash with a sabre. The edge of his hand smashed into the back of Kallan's neck and the sergeant seemed to crumple in mid-stride, then go down like a back-broken rabbit.

"Get him out of here, Magoon," Dusty ordered.

Although he'd never in his life felt less like obeying an order, the big Irishman bent and gripped Kallan's arm. He lifted Kallan to his feet, slipped an arm between the other's legs and draped Kallan across his shoulders. Magoon headed for the door, the rage which filled him against Madlarn not lessening as he kicked open the doors and left the building.

Dusty allowed Magoon to leave before he turned
towards Madlarn once more. The small Texan rubbed
the heel of his right hand against the palm of his left,
working the ache from it. He knew the danger of using
any karate blow and hoped he had not struck too hard.
Kallan was a tough man and should take no harm from
the *tegatana* blow. He had to be stopped and stopped
fast and Dusty did it the only way he could.

Cold grey eyes watched the men behind the bar. Tuck
and Kete stood away from their boss as if wishing to
dissociate themselves from him. They knew who Dusty
was and they could both see the Texan was on the prod.
When a man like Dusty Fog went on the prod it behoved
all who might have crossed him to hunt for the storm
shelters.

"Get out, both of you," he said quietly.

Just as quietly, the two men eased by their boss. Tuck
opened the door and slipped through it followed by
Kete, who closed it after him just as quietly. The ticking
of the wall clock sounded loud in the stillness of the
room.

Standing alone Madlarn felt the cold hand of death
on him. He licked his dry lips and watched Dusty's face,
trying to read something from the impassive face and
failing in his try.

"She kept coming here," Madlarn croaked. "Forcing
herself on me. What could I do——"

Before he finished what he hoped would be a speech
throwing the full blame on to Noreen, Madlarn wished
he'd never started it. The cold grey eyes never left his
face, they seemed to bite down inside him, make his
stomach crawl with fear.

"We done nothing wrong——!" he whined.

Still Dusty did not reply. The Texan's eyes looked
pointedly at the mark on Madlarn's neck. Slowly the
sutler lifted his hand to feel the swollen surface of the
bite.

"You'll be gone from here before nightfall," Dusty
said quietly.

"But this place. I sank——"

Madlarn might never have spoken for all the notice Dusty took of him.

"Sergeant Kallan's one of my men. If I leave you here he'll kill you and I wouldn't blame him in the least. But I'd still have to hold him for a court martial and the whole filthy game'd come out. Even if he didn't hang for the killing it'd break him. He's a good soldier, deserves better than that."

"It might not do you any good, either," snarled Madlarn, seeing a chance by which he might yet get clear. "Not to have it known what's been going on——"

In his rage and fear Madlarn made the mistake of coming near to the bar counter. Dusty's left hand lashed around, the back of it smashing into the man's mouth and sprawling him into the bar. Madlarn snarled in rage, his hand went to his gunless side, clawed at it. Then his eyes went to the double-barrelled ten-gauge shotgun under the counter.

"Go ahead!" snapped Dusty. "Try for it!"

In that moment Madlarn knew Dusty was aware of the shotgun under the bar. Not only aware of it but willing to let the sutler make his play for it. Madlarn became painfully aware that Dusty no longer wore his regulation sword belt with a revolver in a closed-topped holster. Instead he wore the buscadero gunbelt and in the holsters hung a brace of Colts. Dusty Fog's gun-speed and his ability to handle the matched Colts were known to all. The small Texan could let him start his move and kill him in what would pass as self defense.

"You got no right to make me leave this place," whined Madlarn, fear once more crawling over him.

Dusty's right hand crossed his body, the white handled Colt almost seeming to fly from the left-side holster into it. Going into what would become known as the gunman's crouch, legs slightly bent, feet a little apart, body thrown forward to reduce the target, Dusty lined his gun. He held it waist-high almost centrally as he lined it full on the target. His left hand started to drive back the hammer and allow it to fall again, the shots thundering out like the roll of a Gatling gun.

Often Madlarn had heard and joined in arguments as to whether a fanning could be done with a gun and make hits. He had always claimed no man could fan a Colt and hit anything he aimed at. Right now Madlarn learned he was wrong, for Dusty Fog both fanned and hit his mark.

At each hand stroke the four-and-three-quarter-inch barrel of the Civilian model Peacemaker flamed and black powder swirled around Dusty. To the tune of every shot came a crash of splinters of glass, splashes of raw whisky, sprayed from one of the bottles behind the bar. Madlarn stood as if turned to stone, some of the glasses and whisky struck him in passing but he did not dare move. He'd no idea how long, or little, time he spent like that. Actually it was around three seconds from the time it took Dusty to draw to emptying his fifth chamber. For all that to Madlarn it seemed to be much longer. At any moment he expected to feel lead smash into his body and stood waiting for it.

The last shot sounded, slowly the powder smoke blew away and to his surprise Madlarn found himself standing alive and unharmed by the bullets. His legs shook and sweat poured down his face. He stared at Dusty who slowly pumped the empty cartridge cases from the chamber and replaced them with loaded rounds. That Dusty used both hands for the job did not give Madlarn the courage to try and grab the shotgun. It lay under the bar, so near, yet he knew he would never be able to move fast enough to get the weapon and prevent Dusty from killing him with the second Colt.

"You're a lousy, yellow, no-good skunk," Dusty said quietly. "And I'm telling you just the once. Be long gone from here by nightfall or I'll be coming after you and when I come I'm shooting on sight."

A shudder ran through Madlarn's frame. He no

longer looked burly but appeared to have collapsed into himself. Madlarn had seen Dusty in action, seen that flickering half second in which Dusty threw his guns and shot. Even Cato and the other guns hired by Bruno Lewis were far from that class. If Dusty Fog said he'd be back, back he would come and he would not break his word.

With a gesture of supreme contempt Dusty turned and walked from the room. At first Madlarn watched the blue uniformed figure, the squared back shoulders, the back so contemptuously presented. He was being offered a chance. All he needed was the courage to take it. One step would bring him to the shotgun, then he could bring it up, line and fire it. At that range, with a nine buckshot charge, he could not miss.

Only he lacked the guts to make the move. He knew Dusty did not take such a chance blindly. There would be noise as he stepped towards the gun, still more noise as he brought it up and cocked it. One sound would be enough to warn Dusty Fog and the small Texan's turn would be fast, ending with a gun roaring in his hand. Madlarn did not think pure luck guided the shots into the bottles behind the bar. He did not think luck would be needed for Dusty to hit a man-sized mark across the width of the room.

So Madlarn stood without movement as the doors swung closed behind Dusty. Then the sutler raised a shaking hand to wipe the sweat from his face. The door behind the bar inched open and the scared face of Tuck peeped around it. The big man looked relieved to see his boss in one piece.

"What happened, boss?" he asked.

A shudder passed through Madlarn's frame, a shudder he could not have hid no matter how he tried. He turned a white, scared face to the man.

"Saddle me a hoss."

"Going to see Lewis?" inquired Tuck. "Ask him for help?"

"Go saddle the hoss. I'm pulling out of here."

"How about us?" Kete asked, stepping through the door.

"How about you?"

"We got pay coming."

At any other time Madlarn might have taken a different attitude but right now his fear of Dusty Fog rode over it.

"You can come with me if you like. I'll pay you before I go if you don't."

"Will Dusty Fog be back?" said Tuck, throwing a worried glance at the door.

"Tonight."

"We're coming with you."

Dusty left the sutler's building and strode after Magoon who had come to a halt, laid the groaning Kallan on the ground and stood looking towards the sutler's. The big Irishman's look of worry left his face as he saw Dusty come through the door and relief took its place. He stood over Kallan and waited until Dusty came up.

"Thought it'd be best if I didn't go into the Fort carrying Slasher, sir," Magoon stated.

"You thought right. The sentry'll likely think things if he heard the shots from the sutler's."

"Which he won't, way the wind's blowing, Cap'n darlin'," said Magoon.

Dropping to one knee Dusty looked down at Kallan. The sergeant forced himself up on to one elbow and rubbed the back of his neck with the other hand. He gave a grunt of pain and then looked towards Dusty. The hate had left his eyes and sanity returned to them once more.

"I'm sorry I had to do that, Kallan," Dusty said. "But I thought you'd kill Madlarn happen you laid hands on him."

"I would have, sir. Thank you for stopping me."

"Do you want to take the rest of the day off?" asked Dusty. "Go home and see your wife?"

Slowly Kallan forced himself to his feet, rubbing the back of his neck as he did so. He shook his head and winced in pain.

"No, sir. I'd better not see Noreen until I cool off a mite."

"It's your choice, Sergeant."

"With the cap'n's permission," Magoon put in. "About Madlarn and them shots I heard?"

"I asked him to pull up stakes and haul out of here," answered Dusty in a voice which dared Magoon take the matter further.

Magoon knew better. In the few days he'd known Dusty the big sergeant could read the signs and knew when to clamp shut his mouth. Right now was such a time and it would not be wise to cross Dusty.

"I'd like to show you the site I selected for the sabre training area, sir," Kallan said quietly.

"I'll come. Are you coming, Magoon?"

"Yes, sir——" began Magoon, then realized he'd given the wrong answer from the cold look on Dusty's face. "No, sir. I've duties to attend to."

With that he threw a salute which Dusty returned, swung on his heel to head for the gate and give the sentry, who inquired about the shooting, some good and sound advice about minding his own business.

"I never reckoned a lot of things about Magoon until you took over, Captain Fog," Kallan replied. "You were right not to tell him to keep quiet about what he saw. Paddy Magoon'd not open his mouth about it."

They walked along without speaking for a time. Dusty threw a glance towards the sutler's building where, at the corral, Tuck and Kete were collecting horses. It looked as if Madlarn had taken Dusty's words to heart and was getting out while he could, running like a stray cur dog after a whipping. All in all Dusty preferred that to happen for he did not wish to kill the man unless forced into it.

"What do you aim to do about your wife?" Dusty asked.

Kallan did not reply immediately. The man strode along as smart as if on the parade square and with his face wooden in its lack of expression. At last he turned towards Dusty.

"I don't know for sure, sir. I'll have to think about it."

"Sure. It's your decision whichever way it goes."

Noreen Kallan's flight from the sutler's building came to a halt as she approached the Fort. She did not intend the sentry to see her apparent haste and so slowed to a walk. It took a few seconds for her to catch her breath but she was in full control of herself as she approached the sentry. He nodded a greeting to which she replied with a smile that took some bringing.

For the first time Noreen had been caught in the act. She knew Slasher had suspected her of numerous little flirtations, not all of them innocent. Never had he been given definite proof. Strangely, she did not fear his anger, knowing it would be directed more against the man than her. Even more strangely in her own way Noreen loved her husband. She realized she'd never been cut out as a career soldier's wife, with all it entailed in the matter of helping her husband up the promotion ladder. If word of this latest incident got out it would ruin his chances of ever rising higher in rank.

At first she thought of heading for home and collecting a few belongings to aid her in her flight. She knew she must go and go fast before she met Slasher and allowed him to talk her into staying, for talk to her about it he would. So she changed her mind, deciding against the house. Instead she would find somewhere and somebody to help her get away.

To leave Fort Tucker called for horses, it also called for a good-sized escort, as there were many miles of bad country, between the Fort and the better populated areas to the east. She guessed Madlarn, unless dead, would be leaving but she wanted no more of the man.

Just what brought the rushers to Noreen's mind she never knew. It might have been thinking about Madlarn

which recalled the problem of the gold-hungry men to
her thoughts. The rushers, or the right sort of rushers,
were well armed, they had transport and would help her
out, if she had something more than her body to offer in
exchange.

Noreen halted and looked around her. Chance caused
her to halt where she did, looking towards the rear of
the office buildings and the door to Dusty Fog's office.
She turned and walked towards the building, looking
about her. Nobody was in sight so she turned the handle
of the door and pushed. It opened and nobody appeared
to be inside. Cautiously Noreen peered in, the room was
empty. She stepped in, closing the door behind her.

Crossing to Dusty's desk she looked at it. The top was
clear of papers, only an unloaded Army Colt which
Dusty used as a paperweight lay on top. For a moment
Noreen stood uncertain as to what would be her best
plan. Then she went towards the desk and was about to
open the drawers when she heard the party door between the office and orderly room opening. It did not
come fully open and she heard a voice at the other side,
a woman's voice.

"I'll just check if Captain Fog left any paper work he
wants attending to, Corporal," said Joanna Lingley,
for Noreen recognized the girl's voice.

Picking up the revolver Noreen darted to the hinges
side of the party door and stood flattened against the
wall. She knew there'd be no time for her to get out of
the rear door and that Joanna would see it closing, then
investigate, if she tried. She knew the girl helped Dusty
with the office work, just as Joanna helped her father
before his death. Noreen also knew Joanna was going to
want an explanation if she caught another woman in the
office, more so a woman like Noreen who took little or
no interest in the doings of the army.

Joanna did not suspect a thing as she entered the
room. Nor did she see Noreen who was hidden by the
door. Joanna entered the office, closing the door behind
her without a glance at anything but the desk. The girl

walked forward and Noreen, gripping the revolver by its
barrel, followed.

Some instinct must have warned the girl for she
started to turn. Before she could make it or have a
chance to see who followed her it was too late. Noreen
swung the gun up and brought it down again, the butt
thudding on to Joanna's head and dropped the girl as if
she'd been pole-axed. There was little noise, beyond the
low thud and a slightly louder one when Joanna collapsed but apparently the man in the next room had
heard something. Noreen was staring at the girl when
she heard a knock on the door.

"Are you all right, Miss Lingley?" called the orderly
room corporal from the other side.

Noreen drew in a deep breath. If she didn't answer
the corporal would come in and she'd be in worse
trouble. She took a chance on the walls and door dis-
torting her voice sufficiently.

"It's all right, Corporal," she replied. "I knocked
something over."

The reply seemed to satisfy the man for he did not call
again. Noreen stood for a moment looking down at
Joanna, then dropped to her knees and turned the girl's
head to one side. Joanna groaned slightly but did not
open her eyes and Noreen could see no signs of blood.
Joanna's hair, worn piled on top of her head, must have
prevented more serious damage from the blow, even
though she'd been knocked unconscious by it. Yet she
might recover and raise an outcry before Noreen finished her work and got clear.

Now she'd committed herself Noreen became cool
and calm, thinking every move out. First she stripped
Joanna's shoes and stockings, using the latter to secure
the girl's wrists and gag her. Then she rolled Joanna
closer to the desk so that even if she recovered she would
be unable to see who stood at the other side. With this
done Noreen returned to the other side and opened the
top drawers. In the second Noreen found what she
sought.

Despite her apparent lack of interest in the army Noreen knew that copies of the sealed patrol routes would be kept. This was why she took the chance to get into Dusty's office. If she could find the reports she'd have something with which to bargain for a trip to the east.

Taking the topmost papers from the small pile in the desk she read them and knew it to be what she needed. Carefully she arranged the other papers in the desk and closed it again. She looked around the room and her eyes fell on the locked pay chest. She went to it, examining it and wondering how she could leave the impression that somebody tried to break open the lock. Her eyes fell on the empty revolver. Crossing the desk she took it up and went back to the box, inserting the barrel through the curved bar of the lock and straining at it. She left the revolver hanging in the lock and made her way towards the rear door. A thought came to her and she ripped a length from her petticoat, crossed and secured Joanna's ankles, then she went to the rear door. Opening it cautiously Noreen looked out but could see nobody. So she slipped out, made her way across the Fort, keeping a wary eye on the houses of Suds Row.

Leaving the Fort by the west gate she took the trail towards Shacktown, the orders hidden in her frock bosom. She did not know how long she had before Joanna was discovered, but hoped to be able to get a fair start.

Noreen knew this time she'd definitely gone too far and could never return to the Fort again. She felt more than a little sad for, no matter how she acted, she loved her husband and did not want him to be the loser by her actions.

CHAPTER NINE

Beyond the Belle Pourche

Noreen Kallan walked along the main, and only, street of Shacktown. Town was something of a grandiloquent name for there were only four wooden buildings, the saloon, two stores and a smaller establishment which lay back from the street and where dwelled several young women and one older; they catered for the desires of the womanless rushers. Scattered along the street were a few dugouts, made by ambitious rushers who planned to stay safe in Shacktown and slip across the Belle Pourche to snatch up small quantities of gold, then slip out again before either the Sioux or cavalry might catch them. Interspersed among the dugouts and wooden buildings were tents of other rushers. Once, not too many days ago, there had been a much larger number of citizens in Shacktown but since Dusty's patrols began their vigorous operations many men have pulled up stakes and headed for some area which did not have such efficient policing.

Walking slowly along the street Noreen kept both eyes open for the sort of men she wanted. She was no fool and meant to see that the men she selected to help her would be the sort to carry out their word, also the kind of men who dared take the risks involved.

For this reason she ignored the cat-house, although she knew full well what it was. She showed no interest in the stores for their owners were men more concerned with prying gold from the pokes of the rushers than in risking their own necks to fetch it from beyond the Belle Pourche. The saloon never entered her calculations for Noreen knew she could expect no help at all from Lewis. He would like the information she carried, there was no doubt of that, but he would not arrange for her to benefit by it.

Noreen had almost reached the end of the town when she saw what she wanted. There were five men in the party and from the look of things were all set to either make a try at running the patrol blockade, or head out for pastures new. Whatever the reason for it the men were packed and ready to leave. She studied the horses of the men, then glanced at the small wagon with its harnessed, two-horse team. Five would be a good number, for Noreen knew there was safety in numbers and five was neither too great nor too small. The men themselves looked like typical hardrock miners who knew their business, not greenhands fresh from the east, filled with the desire to obtain wealth if not the ability to do so.

"Howdy, ma'am," greeted the big, red shirted and bearded man who appeared to be the leader of the party. He removed his hat and stepped forward. "Can we help you?"

"I figure it might be the other way around," she answered, smiling, her eyes flickering from man to man and read their interest in her.

"How d'you mean, ma'am?"

"You've got something I want and I've something you can use," Noreen replied to the big man's question. "So we ought to be able to get along."

Studying Noreen the man frowned. He knew the women at the cat-house and the half a dozen or so girls who worked for Lewis at the saloon. Noreen was none of them, which meant she came from the Fort. His eyes went to her left hand, noting the wedding ring. Then he looked her over, studying the way her gingham frock clung to her rich, full body. The dress was not that of a calico cat or a saloon girl, nor was it what a respectable lady might wear.

"I still don't get it, ma'am," he finally said.

"You boys look as if you're going to try and get across the Belle Pourche."

"Maybe are, maybe ain't," answered the man.

"Be a lot easier if you knew where the patrols are likely to be, wouldn't it?"

Now she had them interested, all of them. They were the sort of men who could find gold, enough for all of them, including herself, once across the river.

"You're right there, ma'am," admitted the big man, as the rumble of talk rose from his friends. "But we've heard as how that new captain at the Fort's ordered his men to play rough with any rushers they catch. I ain't fixing to tangle with the cavalry in a fight when they've got the law behind them."

"It'd be different if you knew how to avoid them though, wouldn't it?"

Noreen could read the interest plainly enough now. She'd got the help she needed happen she played her cards right. Slowly she reached up and pulled the papers from the front of her frock. She opened it out but did not offer to hand it to the man.

"This's the orders for the patrols which are out," she remarked. "With them we could miss the soldiers and get across the river."

"We, ma'am?" asked the big rusher.

"We! I'm not handing this over unless I go with you, both in and east when we've taken enough gold."

A mutter rose from among the men and the big miner, whose name appeared to be Frank, joined the others, sinking to his haunches and talking. Noreen stepped forward and leaned on the side of the wagon watching the men.

"Where'd you get them from, ma'am?" asked one of the men. "They might not be right."

"They're right. I took them from Captain Fog's desk and we'd best get moving before they're missed."

The words brought a further burst of muttering from among the men. One threw a scared look in the direction of the Fort. The others seemed to be in agreement and Noreen decided she'd best hurry matters along.

"Well, do we have a deal, or do I try some of the others?"

Frank came to his feet. "Why're you doing this?"

"Because I want to get away from my husband and a soldier's pay doesn't give me enough to do it," she replied frankly. "And before you ask me, Slasher was a damned good husband, too good for the likes of me. You've got your choice, make it fast or I'm going."

"Let Frank take a look at them reports, ma'am," suggested one of the men.

"Not without your promise to take me along."

"You got my word, ma'am," Frank grunted. "Reckon you can trust it?"

"Sure. I know which way you're headed and unless you take me I'll make such a fuss that others'll follow you and I'll tell Captain Fog where you're headed. So you've everything to lose by not keeping your word."

Holding out his hand for the report Frank chuckled. The woman, whatever her reason for leaving her husband, had a lot of sense and sand to burn. He looked at the top sheet of the report and saw that it appeared to be genuine enough. On reading it through Frank could tell it would do all the woman claimed, show them a way to avoid the patrols. He knew the Belle Pourche well, knew the names given to the various fords and bends by the army. From the patrol orders he could tell just where to go without running into soldiers.

"You got a deal, ma'am," he said, handing her the report. "Come with us as we go in. On the way out we'll run to the east and you can leave us at Yankton if you like."

"I'll ride the wagon, we can talk as we go," Noreen replied. "I don't know what start we'll have but let's make the most of it."

Frank helped Noreen on to the box of the wagon which was driven by the youngest member of the party, a slim youth who blushed furiously when she smiled at

him. The others mounted their horses and Frank waved
the wagon to start. He took the point of the patrol himself and headed away from the town.

Knowing they'd been watched by some of the nearby
rushers Frank did not go in the direction he'd decided
on at first. He used much the same tactics as the cavalry
patrols in that he kept a careful watch on the back trail
until out of sight of the town. Then, when sure nobody
followed, Frank swung his horse and led the others way
to the north, making for an area the cavalry patrols did
not cover.

Watching the range slip by Noreen felt emotions
churning inside her. She hated herself for what she'd
done. It seemed that ever since she'd met him she'd
spoiled Slasher's career and now she'd done this. It was
something of a relief to know that Captain Fog would
not blame Slasher for her actions. In time she would be
forgotten and her husband could mend the career she'd
spoiled.

To get rid of the thoughts Noreen turned to the young
man but as a conversationalist he proved to be a failure
for he blushed and stammered, his sole topic being to
gasp, "Shucks ma'am," whenever she spoke.

So Noreen felt pleased when Frank brought his horse
around and came to ride by her side. He looked up at
her for a moment as if trying to sort out his words, then
finally he asked:

"Everything all right?"

"Sure," she answered, watching one of the other men
taking the point as scout. "My name's Noreen. Say, I'm
not a bad cook, so I'll do all the cooking and maybe
some washing and clothes mending, that'll make up for
my not being much use at digging."

"That'll set well with the boys. It's been some time
since we tried any woman's fixings."

"How much further to the Belle Pourche?"

"About seven miles to the crossing we want. We
aren't going the straightest route though."

"No, that wouldn't be wise."

"There's a patrol due back today and I reckon the way we're going ought to let us miss them."

Noreen looked around the side of the wagon, peering into the distance. She almost hoped to see the rising dust which would tell that the papers were missed and a patrol was after them. Behind she could see nothing at all but the range, the rugged country through which they travelled did not offer chances of seeing, or being seen from any distance.

"You reckon your husband'll be after you?" asked Frank.

"Maybe. If he's any sense he'll let me go, I'm trouble for him, Frank."

"I don't reckon you could be trouble for any man," Frank replied, his eyes on her face.

She shook her head. "Don't count on it. Once across the Belle Pourche and back with the gold you'll show good sense if you leave me at Yankton."

"Never was one for showing good sense."

The words disturbed Noreen. She did not want trouble among the men and she knew it might come unless she watched her step every minute of the time. Noreen did not know which would be her best bet, let the others know from the start that she was Frank's woman, or keep them all at bay.

The thoughts kept Noreen occupied, that and talking with Frank, until they saw the water of the Belle Pourche ahead. Frank showed that he was not exactly unaware of the danger which they found themselves in. He left the wagon and the others hidden in a draw while he rode down to the river and made a thorough scout of the banks. He'd brought them to the area he wanted and almost directly to a ford he'd known about and hoped to try, but could not, due to the danger of being caught by a cavalry patrol. This day he could cross in safety for there were no patrols in the vicinity.

Taking off his hat Frank waved it around his head and the rest of his party moved forward. On the wagon box Noreen watched them drawing ever nearer to the river. Her every instinct told her she could still go back, but once across the Belle Pourche it would be too late. She steeled herself, gripping the side of the jolting wagon as it made for the ford.

"Get your ropes on the wagon, boys!" yelled Frank. "The bottom's sand and it might stick."

For all their worries on that score the crossing was made with little difficulty and Frank told them to hide on the Sioux's side while he scouted around once more. The others let him go, knowing they could trust him and could rely on his judgment to pick a good spot for their efforts.

Inside fifteen minutes Frank returned with news that he'd found a spot which might suit their needs. The others followed, although now they showed much caution for they'd passed beyond the control of the United States cavalry and were in the land of the Sioux. If the Sioux caught them death would be preferable to what they would get.

"Trust ole Frank to pick the right kind of place," remarked one of the men as they approached the spot which Frank selected for their mining operations.

Noreen looked down at the small stream, one of many which fed the Belle Pourche. It wound along the floor of a small valley, the bushy slopes of which offered good cover for them. Frank ordered the young driver to take the wagon to a small clearing on the edge of the stream, where they could make their camp and wash the gold from the gravel and riffles of the stream.

The oldest member of the party jumped from his horse and gave a broad grin as he looked at the others.

"I can smell the gold from here," he said excitedly. "Let's get to washing it, boys."

"Yeah, we don't want to stay here any longer than we can help," agreed Frank. "We'll wash gold all today and maybe tomorrow, then we'll slip out in the dark."

He helped Noreen down from the wagon and she looked around her. "Where do I start cooking?"

"You don't until after dark," he answered. "Then

you'll have to do it over as small a fire as you can manage.''

The men were unloading the wagon, working fast as they dug out their gold pans and shovels. Noreen stood by the side of the team and wondered what was happening at the Fort. She hoped Joanna Lingley had been discovered and was not too badly hurt.

So busy were the men with their work and Noreen with her thoughts that not one of them paid the slightest attention to the shrill whistling of birds among the bushes.

Back at Fort Tucker, Joanna recovered from the blow on the head. It took her a few moments to settle the spinning in her head. She tried first to put a hand to her head and felt the bonds around her wrists. Then it struck her that something was in her mouth. She tried to shove it out with her tongue and failed, so she started to struggle. That was when she discovered her ankles as well as her wrists were secured.

For a moment Joanna struggled without success. A thought came to her and she rolled from her side on to her back. Lifting her legs she brought them down hard, hoping to make enough noise to let the corporal in the orderly room know of her predicament. All she did was bruise and hurt her heels for her shoes had been removed. Joanna did not try again.

In desperation Joanna started to roll across the floor. It hurt her but she reached the party door beyond which lay the orderly room. Wriggling around she lay with her feet against the door. She lifted her legs and kicked as hard as she dared, bumping the door. Three times she tried before she remembered the next room would be empty. On her arrival McTavish, the corporal of the orderly room, had mentioned that he'd much work to do at the Quartermaster's branch and would be out for the rest of the day.

Joanna lowered her feet in frustration and lay for a moment flat on her back. She did not know how long it might be before she was rescued and so tried to get herself as comfortable as possible.

From the way things went Noreen Kallan had a lot of luck after her flight from the sutler's building. There was the delay while Dusty dealt with Madlarn and Kallan recovered. Then the men did not come straight to the Fort but went around it as they talked of Noreen's future and of things which would take Kallan's thoughts from his wife's disloyalty.

Her luck held in that she narrowly avoided being seen by the two men as they crossed the winding track leading to Shacktown on their way to look over an area Kallan wished to lay out as a sabre training course. So with one thing and another Noreen was crossing the range towards the Belle Pourche as Dusty and Kallan entered the Fort.

After dismissing Kallan to go home and see what he could arrange with his wife, Dusty headed for his quarters instead of the office. He went along to his room and found his striker cleaning boots, so he left the man to it. Hearing laughter from the room shared by Mark and the Kid he opened the door and entered.

Seated around the small table, playing poker for chips, were Mark, the Kid and Gilbey. The latter came to his feet smartly but Dusty waved him down and looked in disgust at the two Texans. He saw something like disapproval in their eyes as they returned his looks and wondered what he'd done to deserve it.

"You're sure a hard boss, Dusty," Mark drawled.

"Allus has been as long as I've known him," grunted the Kid.

"What's all that about?" asked Dusty.

"You know what it's all about," Mark stated. "You knowed well enough we fixed it with Joanna to go out and see if we could down a couple of turkey cocks we've seen on the range."

"Should've been gone by now," agreed the Kid. "Only she said she'd go down to the office and see if you'd got any work for her. I told her, 'Gal,' I said,

'you-all keep clear of that Dusty, 'cause even if there
no work to do he'll find you some. He just can't bear
seeing folks not working.' And I was right.''

"The next time you're right about anything'll be the
first," Dusty grunted. "Anyhow, what the hell are you
pair blaming me for? I've not been near the office since
morning muster and there wasn't a thing for Joanna to
do even if she went in.''

"She could be showing sense, sir," Gilbey remarked.
"Keeping well clear of Texans and such fool cr——''

The words trailed off unsaid as Gilbey remembered,
not quite in time, that Dusty was also a Texan. Gilbey
saw the tolerant grin which came to Dusty's face.

"Was I to put you on another week as officer of the
day you'd reckon I was pulling rank to get my revenge,
mister.''

"Who me, sir? I learned better than say a thing like
that when I was a green shavetail.''

"You've been teaching to Jarrow and Cardon,"
grinned Dusty. "I can't get more than a yes or a no
from either of them half the time.''

By hard work and proving himself willing to learn
and to make up for his previous slackness, Gilbey had
come to the point where he could exchange polite banter
with Dusty at such times. It gave the young lieutenant
some pride when he did so, for he wanted Dusty to have
a good opinion of him.

"Do you reckon Joanna could've gone home and
forgotten about the hunting?" asked Dusty.

"That's about as likely as me voting Republican,"
drawled the Kid. "Which same's not likely at all. You
know her as well as we do, Dusty. Can you see her missing a chance to hunt down a couple of fat ole turkeys
that'd look good in the oven!''

"Come to think of it I can't," admitted Dusty. "I'll
walk down to the office and see what's she found so interesting to do. Do you feel like stretching your legs instead of wasting your life in gambling and corruption,
Mr. Gilbey?''

Such a question by a senior officer could only be met
with the affirmative whether the junior wished to stretch
his legs or not. However, Gilbey was, like all the officers
and sergeants of the Fort, always willing to accompany
Dusty, for there was usually something the small Texan
could give his knowledge and wisdom to and a man
could learn plenty just by listening to him.

So Gilbey and Dusty walked from the officers' quarters and headed for the office. Dusty did not mention
anything that happened at the sutler's building but told
Gilbey of the plans for the sabre fighting course. They
reached the rear door of the office and Dusty opened it.

The first thing which Dusty saw was the revolver
thrust into the clasp of the pay chest padlock. Then his
eyes went to the desk where Joanna's bound feet waved
in sight around the edge. The girl had heard the door
open and started to attract attention to herself the only
way she could.

Dusty crossed the room fast and dropped to his knees
beside the girl, taking a clasp knife from his trousers
pocket and cutting through the knot of the gag. Gilbey
was by his side and bending to try and unfasten
Joanna's wrists.

"Where's McTavish, Mr. Gilbey?" Dusty snapped.

"Working on the accounts with the Quartermaster-
sergeant. Are you all right, Joanna?"

For a moment the girl did not reply. Her jaws ached
from the grip of the gag and as her legs and wrists were
freed she felt the pins and needles pricking off restored
circulation. Tears of pain trickled down her cheeks and
it took her a lot of effort to get control of herself.

Helping Joanna to rise Dusty supported her to a chair
by the desk and placed her in it. He threw another
glance at the lock then looked up at Gilbey.

"Get some water, the Sergeant-major and McTavish,
please Mr. Gilbey."

After Gilbey left the room Dusty went to the box and
looked at the revolver. He recognized it straight away as
the unloaded Army Colt he used as a paper-weight.

Dusty examined the lock, making sure it had not been damaged by this crude attempt to open it. He removed the revolver and returned to the desk where Joanna sat holding her jaw, working it from side to side as if she'd been hit on it.''

"Take it easy, gal," he said gently. "Are you all right?"

Joanna felt at the bump on her head, winced and then answered, "I will be in a few minutes."

"What happened?"

"That I don't know. I came in to check if you'd left any work. Walked through the door and that's all I remember until I recovered and found my hands and feet tied and that gag in my mouth."

Gilbey came back at that moment, the pitcher of water in his hands. He poured Joanna a drink and she took it eagerly.

"Hogan and MacTavish are outside, sir," he said.

Taking the key to the pay chest from his pocket Dusty told Gilbey to check on its contents. The young lieutenant did as ordered, reporting that everything was all right. Dusty expected this for he did not think anybody could have forced the lock in such a manner. After locking the chest again Gilbey handed Dusty the key and left the room to return, followed by the orderly room corporal.

"You saw Miss Lingley come into my office?" asked Dusty.

Looking distinctly uneasy MacTavish nodded. He did not know what might be wrong but was sure that something was. He glanced at Joanna's dishevelled appearance and bit down the questions he would have liked to ask.

"What happened then?" Dusty went on.

"I was all set to go to the quartermaster's branch, sir. Miss Lingley's been in your office, helping with the paperwork often enough so I left her to it. I thought she was all right. She said she was, right after she knocked something over and I called to her about it."

"I never knocked anything over," gasped Joanna. "Or spoke to you after I came into the office."

"But I heard you, ma'am!"

"You're sure it was Miss Lingley's voice?" asked Dusty.

MacTavish gulped. "No, sir. Not certain. I didn't come into the office. But it was a woman's voice and I didn't think there was anybody but Miss Lingley in here so I left it at that."

"Wait outside!" Dusty ordered and the corporal saluted, then left the room.

For a couple of minutes Dusty paced the room like a cougar in a cage. Both Joanna and Gilbey knew he was thinking and knew better than interrupt his train of thoughts.

At last Dusty halted, bent and took up the length of white cloth which had been used to secure the girl's ankles. Her wrists and mouth had been bound by her own stockings but this was of different material.

"Does this belong to you, Joanna?" he asked.

She took the cloth, turning it over between her hands and shaking her head. "No. It's not from my p— mine."

Then Dusty guessed what the mysterious intruder must have been looking for. He headed for the desk and pulled open the drawer in which lay the copies of his patrol orders. He did not need to take them out to know the top one, the routes for the patrols at present in the field, was missing. Nor did he need to think too much about who took them and why.

A woman had been in the room, felled Joanna, tied her up and gagged her. A woman answered MacTavish when he called on hearing either the blow or Joanna falling to the floor. In all the Fort there was only one woman Dusty reckoned would have the need to take the papers.

"Mr. Gilbey, sound assembly. Detail off a twenty man patrol to be ready to ride in fifteen minutes. Get Mark and the Kid here fast."

"What is it, Dusty?" gasped the girl, seeing the way Dusty looked and acted, reading that something was badly wrong from it.

"Trouble, Joanna. Go to your quarters."

Hogan knocked and entered at that moment. "Sergeant Kallan wishing to speak with you, sir."

"Show him in and take Miss Lingley to her quarters."

Although she wished to learn what was wrong Joanna did not argue. She rose to her feet and allowed Hogan to help her from the room. Kallan entered, throwing a startled look at the girl, then saluted Dusty.

"It's Noreen, sir," he said. "She's not at home, or on the Fort."

"I know, Kallan. Sit down."

Quickly Dusty told the man his suspicions and Kallan listened without a word but took the strip of white cloth and looked at it.

"Yes, sir," he admitted. "It could be from Noreen's petticoat. Why'd she do it?"

"I don't know for sure, Sergeant," Dusty answered. "I'm taking out a patrol to try and bring her, and whoever she's using the orders to persuade to help her, back before it's too late."

"Permission to ride with you."

"Permission granted."

Dusty listened to the notes of assembly and waved Kallan into the chair. The sergeant looked haggard and pale under his tan. Dusty felt that Kallan loved his wife and deserved a better deal than he'd been given.

A knock sounded at the rear door, Mark and the Kid stood outside so Dusty stepped out to give them orders in a low voice. Neither asked any questions, for they knew him too well to waste time when that hard, bitter note came to his voice. Without an unnecessary word they turned and headed for the officers' stables to collect their horses. On the square beyond them they saw men form up and Gilbey standing impatiently waiting to carry out Dusty's orders.

"I don't hold you responsible in any way, Kallan," Dusty said as he closed the door of the office. "Go get ready. Tell Mr. Gilbey I said you were to ride with the patrol and that I'll command it."

"Yo!"

Even in his grief and anxiety Kallan remembered his drill and training. He saluted smartly and left the room. Dusty shook his head sadly and then made for the office door.

Gilbey came up at the double after selecting his men and dismissing the rest.

"Detail sent to prepare to leave, sir. Permission to ride with you?"

"Not granted, mister. You'll take command of the Fort."

"Do you know what this is all about, sir?"

"Yes."

With that one word Dusty walked by Gilbey and headed for the officers' stables. Already Mark and the Kid were leading their saddled horses out ready to follow his orders.

Dusty knew how little time there was. Noreen and her helpers would be headed for a part of the Belle Pourche his patrols did not cover. In that area there had been considerable Sioux movement over the past week, which was one reason Dusty kept his men from it. The Sioux would deter any rushers and he did not wish to chance an incident by having soldiers in the same area as the Sioux. He knew Noreen had taken the orders to bribe a passage east. That meant she'd gone with the men who she'd presented with the plans and was heading right into the Sioux on the wrong side of the river.

CHAPTER TEN

Noreen's End

Following Dusty Fog's orders, as they'd done without question ever since they threw in their lot with him, Mark Counter and the Ysabel Kid rode from the side gate of the Fort which led them on to the winding track to Shacktown.

"What do you make of it, *amigo*?" asked the Kid.

"I don't know," admitted Mark. "All I know is that Dusty's tolerable eager for us to find Mrs. Kallan and stop her leaving Shacktown with any rushers."

"Gay gal, that Mrs. Kallan. Danced a couple of times with her that night of the ball. Made me real hot under the collar."

Neither spoke again for a time. Dusty's orders had been brief and to the point, leaving much to be explained, not that Mark and the Kid asked for explanation when Dusty gave his orders. He'd told them to head for Shacktown, find Noreen Kallan and prevent her leaving, or if she'd left try and find out who with and where she'd gone. With Mark and the Kid that was all they needed, why they had to find and hold the woman did not matter, for their boss had given the orders.

The few people on Shacktown's streets paid little attention to Mark and the Kid, for they'd been around enough no longer to be a novelty. The two Texans could see no sign of Noreen on the streets but they rode clear through the town and back to make sure.

"Try in the stores," suggested Mark.

Swinging from their horses the two Texans headed for the first store but its owner disclaimed all knowledge of Noreen Kallan. He looked a worried man and was, for he no longer made a profit and spent most of his time wondering how soon he might be allowed to pull up stakes and go east with a safe escort.

The stores gave no clue as to where Noreen might be and the Texans did not even consider the brothel. Noreen might have her faults but she would never enter such a place, not so near to the Fort certainly. She might have gone into the saloon though and so Mark and the Kid headed towards it.

The Shacktown saloon did not have the charm of Dog Kelly's place in Dodge City, nor did it have size or grandeur of many another prosperous house of entertainment. Rather it had been rapidly thrown up of rough logs, given the minimum of furnishings and opened to haul in as much money as possible for the enrichment of its owner. Even on the brightest of days Bruno Lewis found need of the lamps which always burned. There were no roulette, chuckaluck or faro tables, the sole gambling devices being the decks of cards which could be obtained from the bartender. His supply of liquid refreshment did not cater for those with an educated thirst that sought rare brandy, champagne or other exotic drinks. Instead of man drank raw whiskey, cheap gin or beer. There were some half a dozen painted, flashily dressed girls, but given first choice at the remuda a man would not take any of them if there were others present, as the others would most likely be better looking and younger.

None of this worried Bruno Lewis, who understood the laws of supply and demand. Sure in Dodge, or even Yankton, the standards of his place would have seen him catering for the bagline bum trade. The point was that Shacktown was neither Dodge nor Yankton and his

saloon offered the only such service in a hundred miles.
So he did not need the frills and decorations to bring in
his customers. They had the choice of either drinking at
the Shacktown saloon, or doing without.

On this day when Mark and the Kid came through the
batwing doors of the saloon only about half a dozen
lethargic rushers lounged around a table idly playing
poker and drinking. The other occupants of the room
were the bartender, two of Lewis's gunmen, Cato was
not present, and a couple of dumpy-middle-aged
women known as girls by courtesy only. All glanced
towards the door but none showed either interest or
worry at the sight of the two Texans.

"She's not here," drawled the Kid unnecessarily, for
Mark could also see that.

"Could be in Lewis's office," Mark replied, glancing
towards a door at the right, a door marked private and
beyond which Bruno Lewis was reported to conduct his
private affairs as mayor of Shacktown.

"Reckon we ought to look?"

Mark shook his head, knowing the Kid full capable of
walking across and kicking the door open to find out
what lay beyond it. Instead Mark headed for the card
game and stood behind the players.

"Looking for something, cowboy?" asked one of the
two gunmen slouching forward from the bar.

"Likely," answered Mark. "Any of you gents see a
woman from up the Fort come into town?"

"Which woman, there's a tolerable few?"

Looking over his shoulder at the sneering gunman
Mark held down his first intention, which was to pick
the man up and throw him through the nearest window.
That would achieve nothing and Dusty wanted results
fast. So he described Noreen and saw a flicker of interest on the face of one of the rushers. Before he could
follow it up the gunman spoke again.

"You should try at the sutler's," he said, and gave

a nasty snigger. "Hear her and Madlarn are real frien——"

Mark came around fast, lashing up his left hand in a back-handed slap which sprawled the man to the floor. With a snarled curse the gunman sent his hand towards his gun and froze.

Steel rasped on leather as the seven-and-a-half-inch-barrelled Cavalry Colt left Mark's holster and the ivory butt settled in his right hand, hammer coming back under his thumb even as he drew. He lined the gun down on the scared-looking man and ended any moves he might have thought to make.

"Say it again!" challenged Mark.

The second gunman saw the start of the trouble and thrust himself away from the bar, hand fanning towards his hip. Then he stood very still. The Ysabel Kid did not hesitate. He moved faster than a cougar leaping on a deer and with the same deadly effect. The bowie knife left its sheath, its blade lining on the man's stomach as the Kid went into a knife-fighter's crouch. The man's hand halted in mid-grab for he could see he faced a master with the knife and that the Ysabel Kid could get to him, send the knife ripping home, long before he could clear leather with his gun. Nor did he doubt the Kid would do just that given less than half a chance.

"Any of you seen her?" asked Mark, his Colt still in his hand.

At that moment Bruno Lewis stepped from the door of his office, attracted by the noise. He stood just in the barroom and for a moment fear crossed his face, brought about by recognizing Mark and the Kid. He could have cursed, for at this time more than any other he did not dare risk trouble with the army. True the two Texans were not army but they were known to be close friends of Captain Fog.

"What's the trouble, Rick?" he asked, coming towards the man Mark felled.

"They're looking for Nor—Mrs. Kallan, boss," answered the gunman, getting to his feet and rubbing the blood from his mouth.

A look of relief crossed Lewis's face for he'd been thinking they might be looking for somebody entirely different. Recently, since the rusher trade slackened, Lewis had gone into a line of business he'd been preparing for ever since his arrival. The profits had not been quite what he expected and yet they might be satisfactory provided everything went all right. Things definitely would not go all right if the army learned of his activities.

"Why're you looking for her?" Lewis asked.

"That's our business," Mark answered.

By this time Lewis had walked to the card table and looked at the players. "Any of you boys seen her?" he asked.

His question came less from a desire to be helpful than eagerness to have the two Texans out of his place.

"I saw her a piece back, Bruno," answered the rusher who'd shown interest before. "She'd walked through town like she was looking for somebody. Stopped to talk to Frank Cochrane and his bunch."

"Where at's this here Cochrane gent?" asked the Kid, sheathing his knife and moving back to join Mark, although he neither relaxed nor took his eyes off the second gunman.

"Was camped down the trail a piece."

"Was?" snapped Mark.

"Yeah. After she'd talked with them for a time they got their horses and pulled out."

"Did she go with them?"

"Sure," replied the rusher. "She went with them."

"Which way did they go?" Mark inquired. "Towards the Belle Pourche?"

The rusher grinned slightly. "Now I can't exactly re——"

The long-barrelled Colt pinwheeled on Mark's finger

and slapped back into leather. He threw the table aside, scattering the players, cards and chips. His two hands clamped on the front of the startled rusher's shirt even as he started to thrust back his chair and rise. Mark hauled the man to his feet, lifted him clear from the ground and shook him savagely.

"That help your memory?" he asked.

"Let me go!" yelped the man. He was no weakling but felt like a baby in the big blond Texan's hands. "Sure they headed out in the direction of the river."

Slamming the man back to his feet, Mark turned and walked towards the door. The Kid did not take such chances but backed away. To the watching men he no longer looked young and innocent. Instead his red hazel eyes were cold, hard and deadly and his face had the hard, savage mask of a Comanche Dog Soldier.

"We're going out of here, Mr. Lewis," drawled the Kid. "And we aren't looking for any fuss at all. Call off your dogs."

"I don't know what you mean, Kid," answered Lewis mildly. "We don't aim to cause you any fuss at all."

"Now that's what I call being real sensible," purred the Kid in a voice two shades more savage than a silver-tip grizzly's growl.

Mark and the Kid passed through the batwing doors and for a full five seconds, until they heard the sound of saddle leather creak and horses walking away, not one man in the room moved.

"Rick, Beau, come with me!"

Lewis snarled the words over his shoulder as he headed for his office. The two gunmen followed him and at the door he turned to tell the bartender to give drinks all round. Then Lewis entered his office, the gunmen followed and he slammed the door behind him.

"What happened?" he snarled, looking them over.

"Those Texans come in asking about Noreen Kallan," replied the man called Rick, speaking with difficulty, for his mouth appeared to be badly swollen.

"So I made a joke about her and Madlarn and the big one hit me."

"He didn't hit you hard enough," snarled Lewis bitterly. "You stupid fools, don't you know what Cato's doing right now?"

"Yeah," came the sullen reply. "We know."

"Then why in hell didn't you just let them ask their questions and leave?"

"I thought we'd throw a scare into them," Rick answered.

"Scare them?" scoffed Lewis. "That's a laugh. If they're half as scared as you pair looked they'd be scared all right. I don't want the army fussing in here."

"They're not army."

"They work for the army and they're Dusty Fog's pards."

At that moment there was a knock at the door and a bartender entered. He jerked a thumb over his shoulder and they heard horses on the street outside.

"There's a patrol coming through the town, boss. Got Captain Fog in command and them other two Texans have joined it."

"Thanks, Joe," replied Lewis, fighting to hide his fear and concern at the words. "Hope they enjoy the ride."

When the door closed Lewis turned to his two men, saw the worry on each face and knew he had better stop it. He thought fast and came up with the right answer to the incident in the saloon and the patrol.

"It looks like Noreen's caught out," he said. "She must have learned where the patrols are and got Cochrane's bunch to take her with them."

"Yeah, they was headed for the east, not the Belle Pourche," Rick agreed. "I heard them talking about it."

"What about Cato?" asked the other gunman. "He's over the river right now and they're headed for it."

"I know that," snapped Lewis. "That stupid, man-crazy whore. Why the hell did she have to pick this time to get caught out?"

"Want for me to go and see Madlarn?" asked Rick.

"No. That side of the game's done now. Anyway, he'll either be dead or running by now, or I don't know him. We'll just wait until Cato gets back with the gold for the goods, then we'll close this place and head east. I don't reckon it's worthwhile staying on here any longer."

Thinking of the goods Cato traded with the Sioux and what he took in payment for them the gunman was inclined to agree with his boss.

On leaving the saloon Mark and the Kid took their horses and rode back towards the Fort. They saw Dusty bringing the patrol towards them and halted their horses until he came.

The patrol rode in pairs, following Dusty was Corporal Dunbrowski, acting as the guidon carrier. That meant not only did he carry the company guidon but he also served as runner, delivering any messages from the captain to the rest of the command. Following Dunbrowski, riding stiff-backed and wooden-faced, Kallan sat his horse and his brooding eyes scanned the range ahead, hoping against hope to see his wife. Then came the twenty men, riding in pairs, each man with his carbine booted under his leg and his percussion-fired Army Colt in its holster. Not one of them knew why they'd been turned out in such a hurry. They did know one thing, that every one of them appeared to have been selected because he possessed a good horse, for the pick of the Fort's remounts were being used on the patrol.

After allowing the patrol to ride by, scanning it for anything which might not meet with Captain Fog's approval, Sergeant Paddy Magoon turned his big bay and rode fast along the line towards its head. Like the others he did not have an idea what they might be doing on the patrol but unlike the rest he did not care. That Captain Fog gave the order was enough for Paddy Magoon.

However, on reaching Dusty's side Magoon could not resist saying, "Could the sergeant ask what we're doing on patrol, Cap'n darlin'?"

Lowering his voice Dusty told the big Irishman what had happened, keeping nothing back. It said much for Magoon's poker playing ability that he neither showed any surprise nor even glanced back at the silent and sombre form of Slasher Kallan who followed them.

"The hell you say," growled Magoon. "We'll have to try and bring her back afore she gets into real bad trouble."

"She's done that already," answered Dusty grimly. "I can't pass over her breaking into the office or taking the reports."

"It'll mean her being sent back to the Regiment and likely the finish of Slasher, sir," Magoon pointed out.

"That's the hell of it."

By now they were riding through the street of Shacktown and most of the people turned out to see them, although there was little or no waving, for the army was not especially well thought of at that time in Shacktown.

Throwing a glance at the two women who stood on the porch of the saloon Magoon could hardly restrain a shudder. It was the first time he'd seen them in the unflattering light of day.

"Saints preserve us," he gasped. "Did you get a look at those two old biddies, Cap'n darlin'? They look even worse than I thought they would."

At any other time Dusty might have found some comment on Magoon's taste and morals but he did not feel in a cheerful mood. He was thinking of the outcome of this business. When he'd spoken about Kallan and his wife's trouble on their return to the Fort he'd been speaking as he would if he'd held a commission in the army. Now he could see that he must not take any action. He could not keep up the pretence of being army over such a serious matter.

Without needing to be told what to do Mark and the Kid fell into line on either side of Dusty. "She left town with a bunch," Mark said.

"Likely that's where they've been camped ahead there," the Kid went on, indicating the area in which Frank Cochrane and his partners had camped.

"Look it over," said Dusty.

Riding forward the Kid studied the camp site for a moment from the saddle, then dropped to the grounds. In the matter of reading signs the Kid had few if any equals in the Fort. He read everything the ground held before he turned and went afork the big white stallion in a single bound without bothering about stirrups or holding the reins to steady the seventeen-hand horse.

"Met up with five of them," he reported to Dusty, who kept the patrol moving at an easy pace. "They stood and talked about things for a time, then she got into their wagon and they mounted up. Headed on to the trail here, pointing for the Belle Pourche."

"Straight ahead?" asked Dusty. "They'd run into Mr. Jarrow's patrol if they did that."

Ever since leaving the Fort Dusty had been remembering the orders he gave to the two patrols. He also tried to work out in his mind, from memory of the map he'd so often studied, just where on the Belle Pourche the rushers aimed to cross. The pieces clicked together in his mind, yet the direction taken by Noreen and the rushers did not lead to the unguarded area of their territory. She must have taken the orders to use them in such manner, to get money and transport east by means of ingratiating herself with the group of rushers.

Then Dusty got it. He cursed himself for not having guessed before. The rushers were playing his own trick on him. They were taking the shortest route to the Belle Pourche only in case anyone tried to follow them. Once clear of Shacktown and away from possible following rushers, the party would swing off in the direction they aimed to go.

"Lon," he said. "Take a point. I want to go direct to Pronghorn Crossing."

"Can do it easy," drawled the Kid in reply. "You figure that's where they're headed?"

Not even to his two *amigos* had Dusty mentioned which direction he sent out the patrols. He nodded in answer to the Kid's question and turning his big white the Kid headed out without another word. Relying, as he'd done so many times before, on the Kid's ability to carry the map of a particular part of the range in his head, Dusty followed his pard's lead.

Time passed, the patrol held their horses to a steady trot which covered ground faster than the rusher party had done. More, they were travelling in as near a straight line as the country allowed, instead of winding about to keep under cover and out of sight.

Suddenly, as the men were walking, leading the horses and keeping up a pace which would not have disgraced trained infantrymen, the Kid stopped. He was out ahead of the others, striding along like a buck Apache, the big white following on his heels like a well-trained hound-dog. He came to a halt, standing still and his head turning slightly to catch some sound which as yet was beyond the hearing of any of the others.

"What is it, Lon?" asked Dusty, coming up fast.

"Shots ahead there, a couple, but more of them now."

Neither Dusty nor Mark, even though they stood by the side of the Kid, could hear any shots. Dusty raised his hand to halt the rest of the men and Magoon snarled out a warning for silence.

"Yep, shots they are," grunted the Kid. "Let's go."

"Mount the troop!" Dusty barked. "Forward at the trot, Sergeant Magoon."

Kallan was first into his saddle and he rode forward, passing Dunbrowski who was riding to take his place behind Dusty. The young corporal showed his quick grasp of the situation by holding his horse back a little. He did not know why they were out still but knew Kallan did not often accompany a patrol, being more concerned with drill training at the Fort.

"Can the sergeant ask what's wrong, sir?" Kallan asked formally.

"Shooting ahead," Dusty answered.

Ahead lay the Belle Pourche, ahead was Kallan's wife and ahead also were the Sioux. Shots coming from ahead meant only one thing. Noreen and the men with her had found bad trouble.

Dusty allowed the men to make better speed now. The horses had blown while being walked and could cover the distance to the river without distress. He did not want his mounts exhausted for they might need some speed later, so he gauged the pace as best he could.

It was several minutes before any of the others could hear the shots. Talk welled up among the men, instantly quelled by Magoon's angry orders. The men fell silent and each gave his full attention to keeping his horse going.

Ahead lay the Belle Pourche River, they all knew the spot to be a ford, an easy crossing. The shots sounded from beyond the river and the men expected to be halted at the water edge, for they were allowed to cross the Belle Pourche only in the most dire emergency and rescuing a bunch of fool rushers hardly seemed to come into that category to the troopers. They'd spent so much of their time on patrols that any sympathy they might originally have felt for the rushers had long since gone. The men knew the danger stirred up by the rushers who crossed into the sacred Sioux lands and had no love for anybody who went over the river.

So it came as something of a surprise when the Kid

rode into the water and started across. The soldiers expected Dusty to call the black-dressed Texan back and instead he also rode in.

"See nobody lags behind, Magoon," Dusty called over his shoulder as the big paint waded boot top deep across the ford.

The patrol made its crossing with no trouble and on the other shore Dusty set a faster pace. He could tell from the shooting and now from the yells of the Sioux that the fighting was still going on. They might yet be in time.

Raising his hand Dusty gave the signal for more speed and the horses responded, urged by their riders. In the lead Dusty rode grim-faced and unspeaking. Mark at his right and the Kid at his left as they'd been more than once in dangerous situations.

The sound of the shots drew nearer all the time, the horses were striding on at a better speed but Dusty still held them from the final gallop which might be the difference between life and death.

While still riding at the same speed the Kid suddenly bent, jerked out his yellow-framed old Winchester. It flowed to his shoulder and he appeared to fire with no pause to take careful sight. Not one of the following men could have said at what the Kid fired until a buckskin-dressed shape slid from a stunted tree ahead and dropped to the ground in a limp pile, a rifle falling unheeded from its hand. Even in the short time it took to reach the tree, the Kid found time to boot his old yellow boy once more. Gripping the saddlehorn in one hand he swung down, hanging over the flank of the big white and scooped up the rifle from the side of the dead Sioux, noting in passing the man wore no feathers or signs of tribal prominence, but appeared to be a run of the mill young brave. The rifle taken up by the Kid attracted his interest. The first thing he saw was that it appeared to be of all steel construction instead of having the brass frame of the old model of 1866. The Kid was well aware that the new model Winchester as carried by Dusty and Mark was made of all steel instead of a mixture of steel and brass. Which meant the Indian had a near enough new Winchester '73, or did have until he made the mistake of shaking a branch in a direction which did not agree with the wind.

Dusty raised his hands shoulder high and held them out from his sides. The patrol caught his sign and knew all too well what they must do. The left file fanned out beyond the Kid and the men in the right-hand file spread out until they rode in a line stretching from Mark to Magoon, who held the flank.

"Draw pistols!" Dusty ordered as they raced their horses up a gentle slope beyond which the sound of shots rose loud and the yells of the Sioux rang out.

On topping the ridge the men saw why they'd been brought from Fort Tucker, although most of them still did not see why they'd broken the treaty and crossed the Belle Pourche to rescue a bunch of rushers.

Throwing a look at the camp in the clearing Dusty saw they'd only just come in time. The wagon stood where it had been halted, one horse dead and the other two struggling against the harness which held it. Two of the rushers lay sprawled on the ground away from the wagon and only one gun seemed to be firing from under it. Of Noreen there was no sight but more than one shape lay under the shadow of the wagon and one of them must be her.

There was no time to think of anything but the Sioux. Dusty saw it to be a small party, not more than a dozen braves, although five out of the dozen had rifles and seemed to possess ammunition to spare from the appearance of the wagon and the way they threw lead at it.

So intent on their prey were the Sioux, as they went into attack once more, that none of them paid any attention to the thundering hooves of the cavalry horses. Then, even as Dusty roared out an order which brought a crashing volley of shots, one brave turned and howled

a warning. The hail of lead slashed into and around the
Sioux, two braves went down, another clutched a
wound but it took a very accurate, or lucky, shot to hit
with a revolver from the back of a fast running horse
and no other damage was done. The Sioux who could,
sent their horses racing by the wagon and one fired a
final shot. Dusty saw the man with the gun jerk and
then go limp as the lead struck him.

The Sioux did not halt but sent their horses dashing
into the bushes and away. Dusty knew better than to
allow his command to follow so he roared an order to
bring all but the Kid and Mark to a halt. They followed
the departing Indians up the other slope, guns out and
watchful for a chance ambush.

Before the big paint even halted Dusty left the saddle
and lit down running, but fast as he moved, Kallan
reached the wagon first. The sergeant dropped to his
knees and a low moan came from his lips.

Noreen lay on her back, she'd been pulled into the
shelter of the wagon but hadn't needed it for she'd been
hit in the back by a bullet which must have smashed
through her heart and come out at the front.

One look told Dusty there was nothing he could do.
He glanced around and saw that already Magoon was
forming up the men and Dunbrowski was checking to
make sure nothing could be done for the two rushers
killed away from the wagon. It only needed one glance
to show they were well past all aid.

Without looking at Kallan, who had drawn Noreen's
body from under the wagon and knelt cradling it in his
arms, Dusty gave orders.

"Two men to unload everything from the wagon,
Magoon! Dunbrowski, take as many men as you need to
clear the harness off that dead horse and put one of our
mounts in its place. Good man, soldier, calm that horse
down."

The last words were to a private who had left his
horse and was holding the reins of the terrified team

horse, trying to calm it. Dusty saw men leaping to obey his orders. Then he saw Mark and the Kid coming back in a hurry. They brought their horses to a rump-scraping halt and both jumped down.

"They've got *amigos* coming, Dusty," drawled the Kid, throwing a look at Noreen's body, then at the wagon. "How about this lot?"

"All cashed, got the last as we came in," Dusty answered, looking under the wagon. "Move it, men. We've got to get out of here."

"Yeah and fast—or stay here for good," finished the Ysabel Kid.

CHAPTER ELEVEN

We've a Gun-Runner at Work

"Get back and watch the Sioux, Lon!" Dusty barked and his pard went afork the big white in a bound, heading the horse to a place where he could see the approaching Sioux.

Dusty threw a look at the cursing men who were trying to clear the harness from the dead horse. He doubted if they would have time. There was another thing to consider. Not one of the cavalry horses had ever been used in harness and would not take kindly to it now. Yet the bodies must not be left for the Sioux to mutilate, he knew he could not allow that.

"Asking your pardon, Cap'n" said Magoon, stepping up and saluting. "But I don't reckon we can take the wagon with us."

"That's what I think," Dusty replied. "Get the bodies aboard it, Sergeant."

Thoughts raced through Dusty's head. He must prevent the bodies, especially Noreen's from being hacked to pieces by the Sioux. Yet he could not stay and fight to try and protect them. Already he'd exceeded his orders by crossing the Belle Pourche in pursuit of the rushers. He could not make matters worse by staying to make a fight of it and feeding further the flames of hatred Crazy Bear and his white-man-hating lodge brothers stirred among the Hunkpapa.

The men left the dead horse and flung themselves to

the task of carrying the five dead rushers to their wagon,
putting them inside. Under Dusty's orders more of the
men threw in blankets and anything which would burn.
The soldier who'd managed to quieten the horse was
now unharnessing it, not meaning to leave it to the
Sioux and guessing what Dusty aimed to do.

Striding forward Dusty picked up a can of coal oil,
fuel for the lamps which lay among the rushers' belongings. He took up the can, shook it and heard liquid
splashing around inside. Removing the stopper Dusty
splashed the inflammable oil on the pile of blankets in
the wagon, then splashed more on the sides and canopy.
He tossed the can aside and was about to apply the lit
match when he realized Noreen's body was not inside.

Dusty went to where Kallan still knelt cradling his
wife to him. Laying a hand on the man's shoulder Dusty
spoke gently.

"We'll have to leave her in the wagon, Kallan, we
can't take her with us."

A face lined with grief looked up at Dusty, Kallan
stared with eyes that did not seem to see and ears which
clearly caught little or no sound, or if they did his brain
could not understand them. Mark Counter sprang to
Dusty's side and gently took the woman's body from
Kallan's unresisting arms. The big Texan carried the
woman's body to the rear of the wagon and placed it in.
Still Kallan made no attempt to get to his feet. He'd not
said a word, or made a sound since running to his wife
and even now gave no sign of knowing what danger he
was in.

"Mount the troop!" Dusty roared as the Kid came
racing his big white back. "Magoon, Mark, get Kallan
on his horse!"

"They're coming like bats out of hell, Dusty!" yelled
the Kid. "Fifty or more and all wearing paint."

Mark and Magoon caught the unresisting Kallan by
the arms and lifted him to his feet. They were strong
men and between them they carried the sergeant to his

horse. Even then Kallan did not appear to know what was happening but his cavalry instincts got him into the saddle.

"Move out the troop!" Dusty barked. "Keep them going, Sergeant."

Turning his horse Dunbrowski rode back along the line, took up the loose hanging reins of Dusty's big paint and led it towards its master. The young corporal was once more showing his courage and devotion to duty, for it was the guidon carrier's job to hold his officer's horse, making sure it did not run away and leave the officer afoot. So Dunbrowski rode back, even though he might die for doing it. He gripped the guidon's shaft in his right hand, Dusty's paint's reins in the left and waited, watching the Sioux who came swarming down the slopes, heading through the rough country and the bush towards him.

Without flurry or fluster Dusty took a match from his pocket, rasped it on the seat of his pants and applied the flame to a soggy, oil-soaked strip of cloth. For a moment he thought he'd need another match but the tiny flame crawled up slowly and grew, spreading across the cloth, setting fire to the canopy. Dusty knew nothing short of an organized fire-fighting party could save the wagon now and the Sioux most certainly could not, would not even bother to try.

So Dusty wasted no more time. He turned and ran to where his horse stood and for the first time saw Dunbrowski. The young corporal's face fought to hide its relief and Dusty made a mental note to commend him for his courage. Right now there was no time for that. Not with the Sioux closing in with every second which ticked by. Dusty raced for the paint, hearing the crack of rifles as the Sioux took long range shots at him. He did not hear the bullets and so guessed they were missing by a considerable margin.

Sensibly Dunbrowski had turned the horses so they faced in the direction the rest of the patrol took. Dusty did not use conventional methods of mounting but went over the seventeen-hand rump of the paint in a leapfrog bound which landed him on the saddle, feet feeling for stirrup irons even as he grabbed the reins from Dunbrowski and yelled:

"Get out of here!"

Dunbrowski needed no urging and sent his horse leaping forward alongside Dusty's striding paint. They sent their horses after the rest of the patrol and behind the Sioux charged after them, howling out war yells and looking for the honor of being first to take coup.

"Form into fours!" Magoon roared, checking the first sign of panic. "I'll drop the first man to break rank!"

Not one of the soldiers doubted Magoon's words. They knew he might regard discipline as being something to ignore in barracks, but not in times such as this. Magoon knew he must hold the men in a formation. If he let them ride wild it would no longer be a withdrawal but a wild flight with men running their horses into the ground. Held as a group they could be controlled, made to keep their horses to a pace which allowed each mount to retain something in reserve.

For all his words Magoon felt nervous. He'd left Captain Fog (Magoon never thought of Dusty in any other manner) to set fire to the wagon. He twisted in the saddle and relief showed plain on his face as he found Dusty and Dunbrowski almost up to him.

"Keep them going, Magoon," Dusty barked.

Even as Dusty sent his paint along one flank of the tight held column he heard a yell from the other side.

"Noreen!"

Kallan screamed the word out. He brought his horse to a tight, swinging turn and sent it hurling back towards the wagon over which flames were now licking. Dusty and Magoon also saw, so did Mark and the Kid and all four brought their horses to a halt.

"Keep the patrol going, Magoon!" Dusty ordered.

With an angry growl Magoon swung his horse and headed after his men. Mark shot out a hand to grab Dusty's bridle and hold the paint even as the small Texan was about to go after Kallan.

"No go, *amigo*!" the blond giant snapped. "I'll cut your hoss down afore I'll let you try."

Even as Mark spoke Dusty saw there was no chance of saving Kallan. The man sent his horse straight back towards the wagon. He bent and drew the carbine, sending a shot at the Sioux. Then lead struck his horse and it went down under him but he kicked his feet free and lit down running, still gripping the carbine in his left hand and drawing his revolver with the right.

Clenching his hands so the knuckles showed white Dusty watched Kallan going willingly to his death. The slopes looked to be alive with Sioux and the patrol were hopelessly outnumbered. Without making a pitched battle, one they could not hope to win at that, Dusty could not help Kallan. It would be death to all his men if he tried and an end to any chance of keeping the peace until the army gathered the following year. A resounding victory over the soldier-coats would strengthen Crazy Bear's hold on his supporters and weaken the saner heads who called for peace. It was as easy as that, one man's life against thousands, for thousands would die if the Sioux went to war this year.

Lead caught Kallan, he staggered but kept his feet, shooting down the nearest brave. Three times while they watched Kallan took lead, yet he kept his feet and reeled on. His Colt cracked out shot after shot until empty. By that time he'd reached the wagon. Throwing the weapons into the back Kallan dragged himself up. A barbed war arrow struck him between the shoulders and he fell forward into the blazing wagon, dropping across the body of his wife.

"He's done for!" said the Kid. "Let's get going, we can't do a thing for him by stopping here."

Still holding Dusty's horse Mark started to turn his

blood-bay and the paint followed. Lead cut the air around their heads and they started forward. The three big horses had the legs of an Indian war pony or cavalry remount. With racing strides they drew ahead of the Sioux and caught up with the patrol, much to Magoon's intense relief.

"Keep them running," Dusty said, catching up alongside the burly Irishman. "We'll make a stand on our side of the Belle Pourche."

"Yo!" replied Magoon. "And how about Slasher, sir?"

"He's dead."

"Did he make the wagon?"

"Yeah."

Magoon crossed himself, for he was a Catholic and the early training never left him. With this simple tribute to his departed friend Magoon gave his attention to the patrol.

The memory of that chase would last long among the men of the patrol. They rode their horses with death on their heels, sending the racing animals through the rough bush, down slopes, up the other side, swerving around bushes but always holding their closed formation. The Sioux were shooting but not with accuracy and not one man had been hit when they rode the horses into the water of the Belle Pourche. Churning up the surface, sending spray into the air, ignoring the wetting they got, the men rode across the Belle Pourche's ford. Dusty reached the shore first and he swung down from the paint as soon as its hooves churned the soil on the other side. Jerking the short Winchester carbine from the saddle-boot, Dusty allowed the paint to lope off, knowing the horse would not stray far.

"Dismount, secure your horses, then take cover along the river edge!" he bellowed as the patrol came from the water. "Draw carbines. On the double! Sergeant Magoon. Move them!"

To the accompaniment of yells and bellows of annoyance from Magoon, lashing the slower movers into action, the soldiers dismounted and made their horses secure to the first thing which came to hand. Then with their Springfield carbines in their hands they dashed to find cover along the edge of the river, flattening down in a firing position as soon as they reached a place.

All eyes were on the Sioux as they poured through the bush, making for the ford. Dusty could see the Kid's guess at their being at least fifty was right enough and likely more on hand in case they might be needed.

"Hold your fire until I give the word!" he ordered.

Nearer swept the fast-riding, feather-decorated and wild-eyed braves. In the lead rode a war-bonnet chief, a Winchester in his hand. He brought his horse to a sliding halt as he saw the sight on the other side of the river. Behind him every other brave also came to a halt when they saw the grim-faced men and the lined weapons awaiting them.

It took the war-bonnet chief who led the Sioux but one glance to know he'd carried the chase as far as he could without making a fight of it. Any attempt to make the river crossing would be met by rifle and carbine fire poured on them by men under cover and who could rest their weapons to ensure a better aim.

No man could ever claim truthfully that an Indian war-chief did not know light cavalry tactics. That chief across the river knew the lessons of war as well, if not better, than most graduates from West Point. Not for one moment did he think the soldiers fled in fear before his men. They'd acted as he would have ordered his own men to act under the same circumstances. Outnumbered, in a poor defensive position, the soldier-coat leader wisely decided to withdraw. There had been no panic in the orderly retreat of the patrol and now they waited, with the advantage of position on their side. The chief, it was Crazy Bear himself, a powerful young man who early made his name as a fighting warrior, and gained the trailing war bonnet by his hatred of the white brother, knew he would have selected this same spot to make a stand.

So Crazy Bear did not force home his attack. He could claim it as a victory for his medicine right now. Yet, if he tried to attack, lost men and was forced to withdraw, by that much would his power be weakened. He could boast of how he and his men drove the soldier-coats from their land, sing of how the other white men and their woman fell before his braves. People would listen, they would know why he did not cross the river and his medicine's power be respected.

Whooping out a string of deep-throated Hunkpapa insults at the cowardice of the white brother, even though the white brother had not acted as a coward but as a wise warrior, Crazy Bear spun his horse in a tight turn. He waved the rifle over his head in a derisive manner then headed back to see if there was any loot to be had from the burning wagon. The rest of the warriors also yelled their war cries, hurled insults at the soldiers, turned their horses and followed their chief.

At any other time there might have been some cheering among the soldiers but not as they watched the Sioux file away from the Belle Pourche. They could all see the grim set to Dusty's lips and knew it would go hard on the man who crossed him. Then for the first time most of them noticed that Kallan was no longer with them. In the heat of the retreat from the river his passing had gone unnoticed until this moment.

"Where's Kallan?" asked one of the men.

"The Sioux must have got him," answered another, resting the butt of his carbine on the ground. "What the hell was his wife doing——"

"Mount the troop, Sergeant Magoon!"

Dusty's voice cracked savagely, cutting off the man's words and bringing the patrol to their feet. He turned and walked to where his big paint stood unconcernedly waiting for him. Thrusting the carbine into the saddleboot, Dusty gripped the horn and swung on to the horse. He sat with his head lowered and eyes on the ground, a dull, aching anger throbbing through him.

"March out, Cap'n, sir?" asked Magoon's voice politely. The burly sergeant knew what was wrong with Dusty and knew better than mention it until Dusty spoke.

"March out, Sergeant," Dusty said, his voice flat.

The men formed into twos and rode forward, away from the river, their talk welling up as they asked each other about Kallan and discussed what they'd seen beyond the Belle Pourche. Mark, the Kid and Dunbrowski waited for Dusty, the young corporal sitting back from the other two, his concern over Dusty showing more than the two Texans'. Finally Mark shrugged, if Dusty's temper had to burst it might as well burst on him. He rode the big blood-bay to Dusty's side.

"You did the right thing and you know it," he said.

Dusty let out his breath in a long sigh. He shook his head like a man coming out of a daze. "I reckon you're right. It was one man's life against twenty-four," Dusty answered. "But I hate to think of why he came to die."

"Reckon he didn't want to live with his wife gone," Mark drawled quietly. "Let's go, there's nothing we can do here."

"Reckon not. Thanks for stopping me back there, Mark."

Saying that, Dusty swung the paint from the river and rode after the patrol. He took his place at the head of the double file of soldiers and Magoon eased his horse alongside the paint.

"You did the right thing back there, Cap'n," he said.

"I should've known, guessed what he'd do."

"No, sir. I've known Slasher for a few years now, ever since he come to the regiment. I didn't know, couldn't tell he'd do what he did. He was a damned good soldier and a brave man. Loved her and I reckon in her way Noreen loved him."

"Why did Kallan leave West Point?"

"He never said and I never asked," Magoon replied. "There was the usual latrine gossip about it having to do with his wife and van Druten but I couldn't say yes or no to it and wouldn't want to try."

"Do the men know how he left?"

"They were all too busy trying to save their own hides to see him go I'd say," Magoon answered.

"For the record we'll say he died in action and leave it at that," Dusty stated. "For the rest, I'll see Miss Lingley and ask her advice."

"Aye, she's the smart one is Miss Joanna and can see things that go right by the likes of us. It's maybe for the best the way Slasher and Noreen ended. We might be able to stop most of the scandal."

"Dismount the men and walk for a spell," Dusty said, not telling Magoon the real reason he meant to discuss what had happened with Joanna. That he held this rank under false pretences and blamed himself for the deaths of the Kallans and the five rushers.

Night had fallen when the patrol returned to Fort Tucker. The men put their horses in the picket lines and the Texans led theirs to the officers' stables. They tended to the three stallions then went to their rooms in the quarters. Dusty found his room lamp lit and Dawkins, the old striker, waiting for him. The old man read Dusty's expression, made no comment as he took the dirty and sweat-soaked blouse, then helped draw off the Jefferson boots.

"Mr. Gilbey to see you, sir," he said, answering a knock on the door.

"Show him in and see if you can raise some hot water for me."

Dusty waved Gilbey into a chair and sat on his bed. The young lieutenant was bubbling with questions but he held them back. He sat waiting for Dusty to speak and finally the small Texan did so.

"Is Mr. Cardon back yet?"

"No, sir."

"I'd better tell you what happened then."

Quickly and without wasting words Dusty told the story of the patrol, of what they'd found beyond the Belle Pourche and how Kallan came to die. Gilbey sat in the chair and listened, never speaking until Dusty reached the end of his narrative. Then he rubbed a hand across his face and took a chance.

"You acted correctly, sir," he said.

"We didn't act quickly enough, mister. And I'm to blame for leaving the copies of the patrol orders where they could be taken."

"Nobody could've guessed——"

"Lack of forethought's never been any excuse, mister. Six deaths are the result of what I allowed to happen. I reckon it's right that you know something. I'm not a——"

"The bath's ready, sir, and Miss Lingley wishes you to dine with her as soon as you're through."

The words stopped Dusty just before he could tell Gilbey his correct status in the Fort, that he was an impostor wearing a dead man's uniform. Dusty suddenly realized that he could hardly give himself away without speaking with Joanna and Hogan, both of whom were in this as deeply as he was. He decided to wait until after he'd spoken with the girl.

Gilbey was ready on his feet. Suddenly Dusty knew the young lieutenant liked and respected him. Gilbey was being tactful, not wanting to keep Dusty from a chance of relaxing and throwing off the feeling that he'd failed in his duty.

"Call a meeting of all combat staff in the Fort in an hour and a half please Mr. Gilbey," he said, coming to his feet. "Mr. Cardon should be back by now."

Not until he was seated in the hot water of the bath and soaping himself did Dusty remember the rifle picked up and brought back by the Ysabel Kid. He knew he should go and talk with the Kid but decided to leave it until after he'd eaten. Dusty did not know but his two pards had already decided this for him and he would have been unable to find them even if he'd tried. They and young Gilbey had seen to that by taking an invitation to eat with the family of the quartermaster-sergeant.

Joanna Lingley met Dusty at the door of her house and took him into the comfortable sitting-room. She waited until he sat down and brought him coffee, then closed the door. Like Gilbey, she knew straight away that something was troubling the small Texan but unlike Gilbey she guessed straight away what the trouble was.

Once more Dusty told the story of the patrol. Joanna listened, noticing that he made no attempt to hide what he regarded as his own failure or in any way exculpate himself. He just stated the full facts in a flat and emotionless voice and finished by stating that he intended to tell Gilbey the full story of how he came to be here, then leave the young lieutenant to take whatever action he felt was necessary.

"You're wrong, Dusty," Joanna replied. "Balance all the good things you've done since you came here. Think of the lives which you've saved by holding back all the rushers who failed to get through. You've done something that few men, army or civilian could have done."

"And I've made a fool mistake that any green, wet-behind-the-ears shavetail would've avoided."

"The blame's partly mine," she corrected. "At least, as much mine as yours. I've handled the paperwork and I never thought to remind you about the lock on the drawer. Father lost the keys, or they were lost when he died. He rarely kept the desk locked so I forgot about it."

"I should have locked the office door."

"And she could've opened it, she or anybody in the Fort with a door key."

"But," Dusty said bitterly, "for all that she got in and through it she and six men died."

Joanna stood with her fists clenched. She did not know just what to say or do for the best. She knew Dusty had done his best, she might have mentioned how busy he'd been since his arrival, using it as an excuse for forgetting to lock the desk and his office. She said nothing for she could not remember ever feeling so helpless as she did at the moment.

"What do you reckon I should do?" Dusty finally asked.

"Stay on, keep quiet and do as you've been doing ever since the start. Put a full report in writing to show to whoever comes from the regiment to take over. But first come and eat something. Nobody who knows the facts can blame you for what's happened today."

"How about Kallan?"

"He went back to die with his wife. I've got to know Slasher well. His kind don't toss their grief or their love aside easily. Whatever Noreen Kallan was, Slasher loved her deeply and in her own way Noreen loved him. One day maybe folks will understand what makes Noreen Kallan and women like her what they are. I don't even pretend to understand her. Maybe it stemmed through their not being able to have any children. I've seen her care for babies and play with little children. I've seen the look on her face while she played with them."

"I could've gone back and tried to save him."

"And been wiped out?" asked Joanna. "Giving Crazy Bear the chance he wants to rouse the tribes, by showing how strong his medicine was. That would've been far more stupid than merely leaving your desk unlocked. Dusty, and you know it. Now you don't say another word. Come on in and have a meal."

"But——"

"Captain Fog," said Joanna in a fair imitation of his warning voice. "From one side of this Fort to the other, with one exception, your word is law. That exception is under the roof of a family's quarters. That's women's country. So you get in the dining-room without another word."

Dusty managed a smile at last and went.

"Attention!"

Gilbey barked the word as Dusty entered his office to find the men he wished to see gathered ready for him. He told them to stand at ease and took his seat behind the desk, eyes going to Cardon who held a rifle and looked as scared as a spooked steer in a thunderstorm.

"You all know something of what's happened today, gentlemen," he said. "I don't intend to go into full details until I've finished——what's wrong, Mr. Cardon, and if it's what I think why the hell didn't you go before coming here."

The latter speech was brought about by the fact that Mr. Cardon appeared to be far from attentive. The young officer gave a guilty start and stepped forward, holding out the rifle.

"We had a brush with the Sioux, sir, a small party across the river. They jumped us, I ordered fire on them and one was hit. We took this rifle from his body!"

"How about it, Sucataw?" asked Dusty. "Why'd they jump you?"

"Young bucks, all hot-headed and looking for glory, Cap'n," replied the old scout. "Likely aimed to try and down a couple of the patrol and run their hosses off to show what brave-hearts they are."

Reaching across the desk Dusty took the rifle. One glance told him it was not the usual Model 1866 which a Sioux might be expected to carry. The rifle he held was nearly new, steel-framed, a '73 such as Mark carried. Then he looked up and the glint in his eyes caused Cardon to take an involuntary pace to the rear and stiffen into a brace.

"I *ordered* Mr. Cardon not to interrupt you," Gilbey said, laying emphasis on the second word. "He wished to report the incident as soon as he returned."

Dusty's question died unsaid. He turned his eyes to Gilbey but the young man stood firm, meeting his gaze. Clearly Gilbey thought he'd acted for the best and stood ready to take the consequences.

"I don't see you as a mother hen, Mr. Gilbey," Dusty said quietly. "Don't make a habit of it. No blame is attached to you. Mr. Cardon, relax."

With a sigh of relief the young officer allowed his brace to sag and waited to hear what came next. Dusty gave a grin as he saw this, then jerked his head to the Ysabel Kid, who brought the second rifle forward. Not one of the men had paid any attention to the Kid's rifle on entering the room as he was often seen with his old "yellow boy" across his arm. Only this was not a "yellow boy," it was one of the new model, brass-headed tacks decorating its butt in the Indian manner, mate to the rifle Cardon brought in, with the same style of decoration.

"Winchesters," Dusty growled unnecessarily. ".44.40 caliber can out-range and fire faster than our carbines. The Sioux seem to have them in fair numbers, gentlemen. To my mind it means only one thing." He laid the two rifles side by side on the desk top, his eyes lifting to the faces of the men around it. "We've got a gun-runner on our hands. He's equipping the Sioux with better weapons than we have. Gentlemen, we've got to find him—and we've got to do it fast."

CHAPTER TWELVE

One Gal, One Gun

Silence followed Dusty Fog's words as the men thought of the difficulties involved in finding the elusive gun-runner.

"Might it just be a couple of weapons fallen into the hands of the Sioux in attacks on rushers, sir?" asked Gilbey.

"That's possible, mister. But we saw at least five of them among the small bunch we hit."

"There's another li'l thing, Frank boy," put in the Kid. "Happen only a couple of them had fallen into Sioux hands it wouldn't be a green buck without coup feathers who got one. They'd be handed over to some war-bonnet chief, or a warrior who'd done plenty of fighting."

"Kid's right thar," growled old Sucataw. "With them in the hands of young Sioux bucks it likely means there's more than a few new Winchesters gone to them."

"Then what're the Sioux paying for the rifles with?" asked Dusty.

The other men looked towards him, then at the rifles. A new Winchester Model 1873 cost forty dollars and no gun-runner was a philanthropist. A gun-runner went into his dangerous trade to make money, to turn a good profit for the risks he took. So the rifles owned by the Sioux were being bought, paid for in some way.

"There's gold in plenty in the Black Hills, sir," Cardon spoke up. "General Custer proved th——"

"While admitting that the sun shines through General Custer's pants seat, Mr. Cardon," Dusty interrupted, "I don't see how he's got anything to do with this."

Cardon grinned, accepting the gibe. He was an advocate of Custer, his belief was that the "boy general" could do no wrong.

"It's sacred ground, mister," Sucataw put in. "No Sioux'd dig into the soil there. Not even one trained at a reservation mission school like Crazy Bear was."

"But he'd know the value of gold, Sucataw," Dusty pointed out. "And not all the rushers who've been killed beyond the Belle Pourche would be empty handed."

"Yeah, but how's he getting by the patrols, the gunrunner I mean?" asked Mark. "Or is he operating from somewheres outside our balliwick?"

"We've not entirely closed the river, Mark," answered Dusty. "More than once the patrols have reported men getting across. It's only the bigger groups, the green hands who try in daylight that we've stopped."

"We've seen no wagon," objected Gilbey.

"He'll not be using a wagon," drawled the Kid. "One man on a hoss, with a couple of well-trained packhosses, at night and using some Injun ford, could get in most any time. Even in day, happen he watched what he was doing."

"And slipped by the patrols?" asked Dusty coldly while the two lieutenants look distinctly uneasy.

"Sure. I could do, so could a few men I could name. Sucataw and Rowdy here, knowing the army like they do, could. Any man with a mite of Injun blood could, come to that."

"The Sioux had us spotted for days now, Cap'n Fog," Sucataw remarked as the Kid finished speaking. "They'd help the gun-runner steer clear of us. At least as long as he'd got more rifles to bring them they would.''

The men talked on for a time but none could offer any definite ideas as to who might be running the guns to the Sioux. The meeting broke up late and Dusty was a thoughtful man as he turned into his bed that night.

Never since joining the army had Corporal Dunbrowski felt more like going out and getting drunk. He'd seen the real raw side of army life that afternoon and would never forget it. So he cleaned up and changed into his walking out uniform then headed for the main gate through which everybody must pass, even if going to the Fort sutler's after dark.

Like others who'd left camp for an evening's entertainment he found the building unlit, locked and deserted. So like most of the men he headed for the dubious delights of Shacktown.

Lewis's saloon had a fair crowd in when he entered but he did not join any of the groups of talking, drinking men. He went to the end of the bar nearest to the door of Lewis's office, leaned his elbow on it and moodily accepted the glass skidded to him by the bartender.

One of the saloon workers went to the door of the office and opened it. An angry bellow from inside brought Dunbrowski's eyes to the fast-closing door for the man came out faster than he went in. Even in the flickering moment of the door slamming closed again Dunbrowski had seen something which made him forget his wish to get drunk. He'd not seen much, just a young woman standing in the office. A young woman with long black hair done in braids, in buckskin clothes and calf-high Sioux moccasins. A young woman with a brown face, an Indian face.

Dunbrowski was puzzled. He could think of no reason why Lewis should have an Indian woman in the office and yet his instincts warned him all was not well. He had not been west long enough to tell the difference between the tribes and would not, on so short a glimpse, be able to tell from the woman's dress whether she be Sioux, Crow, Cheyenne or what. Yet his instincts warned him the girl should not be there and he intended to find out what she was doing.

Finishing his drink he put the glass on to the bar top and walked casually from the room. Once outside all casualness left him and he hurried around the side of the saloon, making for the rear doors, one of which led into Lewis's office. He had not been around the rear of the saloon before but saw which was the office by the light in the window. There was no fence around the building, it faced the open range, apart from a small corral in which were the horses owned by Lewis and some of his workers. Through the darkness Dunbrowski could see the horses moving about, but could not make out more than that horses were in the corral.

He reached the window and flattened out by the side of it. Like most of the rooms in the saloon the window had no glass to it and a heavy canvas curtain hung over it. However, the canvas did not fit well and by peering through a gap left by it Dunbrowski could see into the office. He could also hear what was being said.

The first thing Dunbrowski saw was that not one but four Indian girls stood in the room. He saw also that Lewis and Cato stood at the desk, facing each other in the light of the lamp, clearly not agreeing on some point.

"And I tell you it's a good bargain!" snarled the half-breed, waving a hand towards the girls. "One gal, one gun. I know of three macs who would pay us two hundred dollars apiece for these four gals and be glad of more."

Lewis sat down, scowling. On the desk before him lay two buckskin bags. He slapped one, lifted it and hefted it in his hand. The bag appeared to be very heavy and Dunbrowski could guess what it held.

"I can understand this. It's gold and we can use it. But four Sioux squaws!"

"I tell you they're as good as money. Crazy Bear told them to go with me and they went without any fuss. They're only dumb stupid Injun women. They'll do whatever their men folk tell them."

"All right, we'll try it. Madame Flora's been complaining about not having enough customers to make it worth her while keeping the cat-house going. We'll take the gals down there, let her have them. Then in the morning she can get all her gear on to the wagons, hide the gals in the back and pull out for one of the new gold camps."

"I know the one. There's a blacksmith'll take these Injun gals off my hands."

Dunbrowski had heard all he needed to. He thought of bursting into the room and taking the two men but decided against it. This was a matter for Captain Fog to handle and the quicker he knew about Lewis's new business deal the better for all concerned. The young corporal remembered the rifles in the hands of Crazy Bear's warriors and knew who placed them there.

Too late Dunbrowski heard the soft footfall behind him and his instincts reacted just a split second too slowly. He was not halfway around, hand knocking open the flap of his holster, when something smashed down on to his head and he went to the ground in a limp heap. The gunman called Rick holstered his revolver, stepped by the unconscious soldier and tapped the door of Lewis's office. He heard the voice of his boss asking who it was and answered;

"Rick. I caught a soldier snooping back here."

The words brought a hurried opening of the door. Lewis and Cato leapt out and stood looking down at Dunbrowski.

"Who is he?" asked Lewis. "I've seen him before."

"He's the one who carries the flag when that damned

captain's on patrol," Cato answered. "Did he hear anything?"

"Enough, I'd reckon," Rick growled. "I was down by the corral, making sure those Injun ponies were all right, saw him come around the side of the building. He headed straight for your window, so I come up and buffaloed him."

"What'll we do with him?" asked Cato.

"Get him away from here and make sure he doesn't talk."

Saying this Lewis turned on his heels and entered his office again. Cato and Rick exchanged glances, then the half-breed bent and dragged the still unconscious young men erect, bent and draped Dunbrowski across his shoulders.

"Leave it to me, Rick," he said. "I'll see to everything."

With that Cato faded into the darkness carrying the unconscious corporal over his shoulders. Rick shrugged, turned and entered the office to await the other man's return.

For an hour Cato was away. When he returned he carried a bundle of clothes, boots, a sword belt with a cavalry holstered Army Colt on it. "Get this lot burned," he told Rick. "And don't open the bundle."

"I'll take the gun," Rick replied, removing the Tranter revolver from his holster and replacing it with the Colt. "See you took what you wanted."

Cato grinned savagely, dropping a hand to the hilt of the Ames knife which rode at his side instead of the Green River blade he'd worn when he went out.

"A good knife's worth money," he said. "I've always wanted one like this."

"Get them clothes burned, Rick!" Lewis ordered. "Bring those gals down to Madam Flora's place, Cato."

At the brothel Madame Flora did not show any great enthusiasm about keeping the Sioux girls all night. She had more sense than argue with Lewis for all of that, for he ruled her life with an iron hand, knowing enough about her to send her to jail for a number of years. So she asked no questions but gave the four young women blankets and told Cato to make them sleep on the floor of the back room where the meeting was held. The girls obeyed docilely enough and Madame Flora studied them with coldly professional eyes.

"They're worth money," she stated, in answer to a question by Lewis. "Who you got in mind to sell them to?"

"Jew Levi up Besno way," Cato answered.

"He'll take them," she said quietly. "I won't be sorry to get away from this neck of the woods, Bruno."

Much easier in his mind now he'd been reassured as to the saleable value of his merchandise by an expert, Lewis left the Sioux girls in Madame Flora's hands. He headed back to the saloon and was soon in bed in his own room, sleeping without a thought of the dead corporal or the Sioux girls he was helping to sell into something worse than slavery.

He was awakened early by somebody shaking him. Looking up he found Cato standing at his bedside and behind him Madame Flora, looking scared, while Rick stood at the door.

"It's them Sioux gals, boss," Cato snarled. "They lit out in the early hours of the morning. Took their ponies from the corral, let the rest out and have gone."

"Gone!" Lewis yelled, bounding from the bed without a thought for the fact that he wore nothing but a long nightshirt. "You mean we've been tricked?"

"Yeah, either that or——" Cato's face lost some of its color as his words died off.

"Or what?"

"That Crazy Bear. He's got all the rifles he needs. He may have talked the gals into going so he can claim the white man took them and get the Hunkpapa out on the warpath."

"Then get after them!" Lewis croaked. "Get them back or kill them."

"Let's go, Rick," Cato ordered. "The hosses didn't stray far and I've got two of them back."

Lewis watched the men leave the room, he threw a glance at the stout safe which stood in the corner. Then he snarled at the woman to get out. He started to dress hurriedly for the fear of death was on him. Already the dead corporal would have been missed and most likely a search would have started. He wanted to be on hand if the soldiers came to question his workers. Then he aimed to get out of the area as soon as the two gunmen returned and could act as escort for him and the wealth he'd accumulated since his arrival in Shacktown.

Dusty Fog learned Dunbrowski was missing earlier than Lewis heard about the departure of the Sioux girls. He was awakened by knocking on his door and called for the knocker to come in.

Sergeant Granger entered, sabre bouncing at his side as befitted the sergeant of the guard. "Corporal Dunbrowski's absent, sir," he reported.

"Absent?" snapped Dusty.

"Yes, sir. I passed him out last night and didn't see him return. On making rounds at reveille I saw his bed hadn't been slept in. Thought I'd best report to you immediately."

Swiftly Dusty rolled from the bed and pulled on one of van Druten's fancy dressing-gowns. He knew Dunbrowski would not desert and did not intend wasting time in futile conjecture.

"Where'd he go?"

"Shacktown, I reckon, sir. The sutler's building was closed. Madlarn's pulled out from what I hear."

"Wake up Mark and the Kid, Sergeant. Tell them I want them, carry on with your duties."

Granger saluted and left the room while Dusty reached for his trousers and Dawkins appeared with hot water in a jug. The striker was pouring the water in Dusty's washbowl when Mark and the Kid entered the room, still finishing dressing as they came.

Quickly Dusty told of Dunbrowski's disappearance and gave his orders. They made no comment, disregarded the fact that neither had washed, shaved or eaten yet. Both left the room, collected the saddles and rifles, then headed for the stables and their horses.

"We could try the cat-house first," Mark suggested as they left the Fort.

"Reckoned you'd think of that," replied the Kid. "I allow Ken Dunbrowski's got good enough sense to get out of bed and back to the Fort afore reveille."

Even as he spoke the Kid had been looking around him, Indian-keen eyes missing nothing. He tensed slightly, not enough to be noticeable to a stranger, but Mark knew him well.

"What is it?"

"That buzzard," answered the Kid quietly yet grimly. "It might be nothing or it might be something bad."

Following the direction of the Kid's pointing finger Mark saw a buzzard drop nearer the ground in a circling spiral. The bird looked well clear of Shacktown.

"It mightn't be——" he began.

Already the Kid was riding in the direction of the spiralling bird and Mark followed without further argument. They found Dunbrowski lying among a clump of bushes half a mile more from town. He was naked, his throat slit from ear to ear and his head a bloody horror where a scalping knife had done its work.

Dropping from his horse the Kid advanced, eyes studying every inch of the ground. Mark remained in the saddle for he knew the Kid could best handle this alone and he would be in the way afoot.

"Indian work?" he asked when the Kid completed his check of the ground.

"Looks that way. Somebody who knows how to read and hide sign for all that. I can't see a Sioux taking that much trouble to hide how he came here or where he went.''

"Might not be Indians, then?" Mark said, glancing at the scalped head.

"Don't mean a thing and you know it. Us Comanches learned to scalp folks from you white-eyes."

"What're we going to do?" Mark inquired, ignoring the Kid's cold Comanche humor.

"You're going to the Fort to tell Dusty. I'm heading for Shacktown to see what I can learn."

This would be the best idea. Apart from their guns Mark and the Kid had no authority to make investigations. They could do so but Dusty, with folks believing him to have the power of the War Department to back him, as well as his reputation with his guns, would be able to accomplish much more.

"You stay out of trouble, Lon," warned Mark.

In all fairness to the Kid, he did aim to stay out of trouble in town. He'd a suspicion of who might have done the killing but meant to let Dusty make the first investigations and only take more basic and effective action if that failed. Unfortunately he reached the corral in time to see Cato and Rick making a hurried departure, heading towards the Belle Pourche at a fair speed. Even then the Kid might have kept his word had he not seen the sign by the corral. Somehow, or by somebody's hand, all the horses had been turned loose from the corral. Only four of them were not shod and were ridden. The Kid read that in the sign, he also saw that Cato had been studying those same tracks and appeared to be following them.

"Mark means to stay out of trouble in town," he said, stroking the neck of the big white stallion. "So it's all right if we follow them two and likely get into trouble on the range, ole Blackie hoss."

Having cleared his conscience the Kid turned his horse and set off after the two men, for against Cato he harbored certain unproved suspicions and on the range, clear of interference, he might be able to turn them into proven facts. So, with his rifle in his hands, the Kid allowed his horse to follow the two men.

Three miles beyond the town the Kid's presence was discovered by Rick. The man was worried about this pursuit, it might be leading them into a Sioux ambush. Some instinct caused him to look back and he saw the black-dressed Texan astride the huge white stallion. Never the staunchest or most reliable man in a real tight spot and with a good sized guilty conscience to stir him, Rick let out a warning yell, started to turn his horse and drew his revolver.

"It's the Kid, Cato!" he howled and fired.

At any time panic is dangerous. In this case it proved fatal. The Army Colt was acknowledged the finest percussion-fired revolver ever built, yet it did not have the range to make a hit at seventy-five yards and the Kid was all of that far away. A skilled man firing double-handed and from a rest might have centered on the Kid and made the hit but Rick was not good, did not have a double-handed hold or a rest. So his bullet missed the Kid by a good country mile and he did not have a second chance.

The old "yellow boy" flowed to the Kid's shoulder and roared but in range it licked the Colt and in skilled hands could be aimed with some accuracy at seventy-five yards range, even from the back of a horse. The Kid sighted and fired in a fast move and Rick slid from his horse. He hit the ground but did not feel it for he was dead even before he landed.

For an instant Cato thought of flight. Then he saw the way the white stallion moved and knew his own horse would be useless in a race against the Kid's. He flung himself from his saddle, clawing the Sharps Old Reliable rifle from the boot as he went, lighting down and diving behind a rock. He landed rolling and brought the barrel of the rifle out ready for use. Only the Kid was nowhere in sight. He'd left the saddle of the horse and already the big white, riderless though it was, headed into cover where it could not be seen or shot at.

The seconds ticked by slowly as Cato lay searching the ground for some sign of the Ysabel Kid. He saw nothing but knew that ahead of him the Kid was moving, darting on silent feet from cover to cover, getting in closer all the time. Cato licked his lips. He'd Indian blood which gave him keen eyes, but this time he'd met his match, for not a thing before him could he see, only the rocks, trees and bushes of the open range country.

A chance taken glance behind made Cato change his plans. He saw dust rolling up, more dust than could be caused by an army patrol returning to the Fort. The Sioux had crossed the Belle Pourche and were coming to avenge the taking of the girls. Crazy Bear's plans were working.

Cato knew he dare not stay. He came to his feet and darted towards his horse with the Sharps gripped between his hands. The Kid seemed to sprout out of the ground not thirty feet from him. Cato skidded to a halt and tried to get the heavy rifle around and into line.

Held hip high the old "yellow boy" crashed in the Kid's hands. His flat-nosed bullet struck the half-breed in the chest and knocked him staggering backwards. The Sharps roared but its bullet flew wide of the Kid. Then Cato was down and the Kid sprinted towards him.

One look told the Kid he could do nothing for Cato. Another look told him he'd best get away from this place and fast. A shrill whistle left the Kid's lips and the huge white stallion crashed from where it had stood in cover waiting for him. Cato's life blood bubbled from his lips, his body stiffened and went limp but the Kid would not have spared it a second glance had it not been for seeing the knife in Cato's sheath.

Bending down the Kid took the Ames knife from Cato's sheath. A low snarl came from his lips as he recognized the weapon. His theory had been proved correct for it was Dunbrowski's knife and the young soldier would never have parted with it while alive.

The distant thunder of hooves brought the Kid back to awareness of his own position. He threw one look towards the sound and then headed for his horse on the run. It looked as if Crazy Bear had in some way managed to gather the whole Hunkpapa tribe behind him. The Kid estimated at least three hundred Indians rode towards him and they were not coming to make loving talk.

He hit the saddle of the white stallion, bringing Blackie around in a rearing turn and letting the big horse run for Shacktown. If the horse fell and the Sioux caught up with him there would be a hot time in Shacktown that morning.

"Sioux! They're on the warwhoop and coming this way! Head for the Fort!"

Bruno Lewis heard the shout from the street. He heard startled yells and reached the door of his room in time to see his workers, including his second hired gun, headed for the batwing doors. Outside on the street he could hear scared yells and people running, all going in the same direction, towards the Fort.

Turning quickly Lewis headed for his safe, fumbling out the key and unlocking the door. He dragged open the heavy door and inside it lay stacks of money and two large pokes full of gold dust. They were what he'd made since his arrival in Shacktown and he didn't aim to leave without them.

Desperately he took out the money, sticking it into his pockets, the front of his shirt, anywhere he could think of. He heard three crashes, as if somebody had broken something in the barroom but he ignored them. He gripped the two heavy gold-filled sacks and dragged them out. Then he was struck with the thought that he could never carry them to the Fort. Nor could he put any of the gold into his pockets for they were filled with money. He thrust the gold back into the safe, ignoring the crackle of flames and the smoke which came from the barrooms. He locked the safe, for he knew the Sioux would burn his place after looting it. The safe would withstand the heat and after the attack was driven off he could come back to get his gold.

With this thought he ran to the door of his room. Beyond he saw three separate fires burning, each apparently started by one of his lamps being smashed to the floor. The flames were licking up the walls, eating away at the bar. He felt sudden terror, thinking he'd left it too late and that the Sioux had arrived.

The knife missed his face by inches, flying from the batwing doors and sinking into the woodwork. He screamed, twisting to see the Ysabel Kid standing at the doors. Then his eyes went to the knife and he recognized it as the one Cato took from the murdered soldier.

"That's Ken Dunbrowski's knife," drawled the Kid, confirming Lewis's thoughts.

"I didn't kill him!" gasped Lewis.

Even over the crackling of the flames he could hear the distant thunder of hooves and yells of the Sioux.

"Cato did."

"We've got to get out——"

The Kid's rifle barrel tilted down and roared, its bullet kicking a splinter by the man's foot and making him halt even as he stepped forward.

"Why'd he do it?"

"I—he heard—he caught the soldier snooping."

"What'd Ken see that made you kill him?" asked the Kid, keeping a careful ear on the fast-approaching Sioux.

"The girls. The Sioux girls. I never told Cato to bring them!" Lewis answered, screaming the words out.

"What'd you give the Sioux for the gals?"

"Rifles. But they were center-fire and most of the ammunition we sold was rimfire."

For an instant the Kid's rifle lined and his finger rested on the trigger. Lewis rushed across the room and the Kid knew what he must do. Turning, he darted from the saloon. The Sioux were close, already pouring by the first of the rusher homes.

The Kid did not hesitate. He hit the hitching rail in a bound which carried him up and into the saddle of his horse. Lewis reached the door of the saloon, a terrified man who saw his end. Desperately Lewis tried to drag money from his pockets and offer it to the Kid.

"Save me!" he screamed. "Take me with you!"

"I liked Ken Dunbrowski," answered the Kid and with a touch of his heels sent the big white at a gallop towards the Fort.

Screaming pleas for mercy and help, alternated with curses, Lewis sprang from the sidewalk and ran a few steps after the fast moving horse. He knew he would be too late and behind him the screams of the Sioux rang louder.

Lewis turned and screamed. His saloon was blazing well for the Kid had not meant for raw whisky to be available to further inflame the Sioux. Lewis knew he could find no refuge in the saloon or anywhere. He tried to make his legs turn but they no longer obeyed him.

"No!" he screamed at the oncoming Sioux. "Don't kill me! Don't—I didn't take your girls. They've gone back—Don't kill me——"

The rest ended in a single hideous scream. Lewis had been clawing money from his pockets to try and buy his life. A young brave forced his horse ahead of the others. He dropped the tip of his lance and, with a wild scalp yell ringing from his lips, drove the point into Lewis's body. The saloon-keeper gave a single scream, the money fell from his hands as he clawed at the shaft of the lance. Then he was down, the warrior pulled his lance free and the hooves of the Sioux horses churned over the boss of Shacktown, smashing his body into the dirt of the single street that would soon be no more.

CHAPTER THIRTEEN

Crazy Bear's Medicine

Morning muster was over and Dusty Fog opened his mouth to yell an order for the day's patrol to leave. With Gilbey and his men on their way Dusty would be free to investigate the murder of Corporal Dunbrowski. The order was never to be given.

"Dust cloud on the west horizon, sir!" yelled the sentry on the gate.

A moment later a corporal astride an unsaddle horse raced through the west gate, riding straight across the square and leaping down before Dusty to throw a salute. "Folks coming from Shacktown, sir. Tolerable amount of them, look in a hurry to get here."

"Mr. Gilbey, Cardon!" Dusty barked. "Come with me. Hold the parade, Sergeant-major!"

Pausing only long enough to unsling the field glasses from his saddle, Gilbey followed Dusty on the run with Cardon hot on his heels. At the west gate they saw the dust and could tell from the way it rose a fair number of feet churned it up. Dusty was about to order Mark and the scouts who had arrived to go out and make sure what caused the dust cloud. He did not give the order for he knew the Kid to be in Shacktown, or in the area of the dust. So he could wait, allowing the Kid to come in and tell. Yet he could not wait for something else.

"All the horses in the Fort, Mr. Cardon," he said. "Picket them across the parade square."

"Yo," answered the lieutenant and darted away.

It was a simple precaution, getting the horses inside the fence. If the cloud was caused by what they all suspected then no time must be lost. If not the horse gathering could be classed as a drill and would be useful practice.

"Have the alarm sounded, Mr. Gilbey. Hold your company, dismiss the remainder to their posts."

Dusty gave the second order quietly and Giley went to carry it out. By now the Shacktown citizens were streaming along the road into sight of the Fort. They came on foot, some carrying a few belongings, but most just in what they wore when they heard the Kid's warning shouts.

The horses were coming into the Fort fast. Dusty looked back on the times he had run the men through this drill and saw it paying off now in lack of confusion. He'd rehearsed the drill for defending against an Indian attack regularly and the men knew their duties. This time they had the stimulus of it being the real thing for none of them thought the dust to be caused by a herd of buffalo.

By the time the first of the men from Shacktown reached the gates all the horses were inside, being attended to by the handling party while the remainder of the men took their posts.

Joanna Lingley dashed across the square and the other families gathered in a group at the edge. The girl came straight to Dusty's side.

"What is it?" she asked.

"Indian attack. Take the women and kids to the mess hall and barricade up."

One thing he liked about Joanna was the fact that she obeyed orders without question. Dusty watched her hurry back and start to herd the families into the enlisted men's mess hall, where they would have some protection.

"Injuns!" gasped the first man through the gates,

pointing back to the town. "Thousands of 'em."

In actual fact the man had seen no Indians at all and could not say truthfully how many or few they were but fear makes for a lively imagination. He staggered by Dusty and more men were coming with the women. Madame Flora and her girls, the workers in Lewis's saloon bringing up the rear, stumbling and staggering, for none were in any way used to exercise.

"Magoon!" Dusty roared. "Ten men to help in those women."

Paddy Magoon sprang forward, ripping out orders and left the Fort on the run with the men hard on his heels. Dusty watched, then saw the smoke which crept into the air from Shacktown. He could not see so much dust now but what he saw appeared to be very close to the town and he'd seen no sign of the Kid, Lewis or two of the saloon-keeper's hired guns.

Even as Magoon and his party half carried, half dragged the exhausted women into the walls of the Fort, Dusty saw the Kid coming, riding fast. Then he saw Madame Flora pulling away from Magoon's hands, trying to get to him.

"I had to take them girls, Captain," she gasped. "Lewis made me take them."

Dusty made a sign and Magoon allowed the woman to come towards him. Then the burly sergeant ordered the remainder of the women to go to the mess hall and keep from under foot.

"What girls?" asked Dusty.

"Four Sioux girls. They got away and headed for home in the night."

Before Dusty could ask more the Kid came racing into the Fort and dropped from his white stallion, throwing its reins to Mark.

"It's come, Dusty!" he said. "Lewis and Cato've been trading guns for gold. Only last time Crazy Bear got smart and gave Cato four gals for the rifles. Then he must have spread the story that white men had taken them and the whole danged tribe's coming down on us."

"Where're they at, Cato and Lewis?"

"I killed Cato out on the range."

"And Lewis?"

"I don't reckon he could run fast enough."

The reply left a whole lot to be explained but Dusty knew the futility of questioning the Kid further. When Loncey Dalton Ysabel got that tone in his voice a man would have better results talking to a cottonwood tree. Whatever happened to Bruno Lewis was no more than he deserved. So wisely Dusty let the matter lie.

More smoke was rising above the town and Shacktown ceased to exist except as a bad memory. Yet few Indians had come towards the Fort, most of them were busy looting the stores. They'd found the saloon ablaze and so firewater did not come to them in any quantity. Luckily the storekeepers did not stock firearms and very little in the way of ammunition, so that did not come into Sioux hands.

Dusty stood at the west side with Gilbey standing just behind him, Mark and the Kid to his other side. They saw Sioux appear at the edge of the scrub land which closed in beyond the hundred yard wide cleared area surrounding the walls.

"There's around three hundred of them, Dusty," drawled the Kid.

"They've got us well outnumbered," replied Dusty. "Bring your company to this wall, Mr. Gilbey, we'll see if a bold front can hold them back."

All around the walls, scattered along the length, stood groups of three soldiers, their carbines in their hands, pouches of ammunition on their belts. The quartermaster-sergeant and his assistants made the rounds, leaving more .45.70 cartridges by each group. The groups that were spread out for the post were undermanned without Jarrow's patrol. Cardon, running from point to point, took the Shacktown men and shoved them into places, doing his best to give the walls a fair share of the reinforcements. Still it was a pitifully small party and they would be hard pressed to hold back a determined attack by such numbers as the Sioux appeared to be.

"If they attack, Mr. Gilbey," Dusty said, watching the Sioux numbers increased as brave after brave came from the blazing town. "One volley from your men, then scatter them to their posts."

"Yo!" replied Gilbey, then headed to his men to give the orders.

Leaning his elbow on the wall old Sucataw, the scout, studied the Indians. He jerked a thumb towards the group of old man chiefs who sat their horses to one side. Dusty stood by the scout now and followed the direction indicated.

"That there's Eagle Catcher on the big black," said Sucataw and pointed to the main chief, a tall, straight old man with a decorated Henry rifle across his arm. Then the scout's finger stabbed towards a tall warbonnet chief in the center of a group of young braves who wore the war medicine. "That's Crazy Bear. Him and the bunch around him are lodge brothers and they're the cause of this trouble. Give Eagle Catcher half a chance and he'd back out right now. Only Crazy Bear's got too much pull. His war medicine's good and folks allus listen to a success, Injun or white alike."

Already Dusty was thinking. He knew his command had little chance in an open fight against the Sioux. They might defend the walls for a short time, then retreat to the buildings he'd selected for defense but the weight of numbers would crush them down. They'd be burned out, slaughtered and the flagging spirits of the hostile tribes would have a boost to keep them going.

Bitterly Dusty blamed himself for it all. If he'd had the sense to lock his desk Noreen could never have got the patrol reports. Then she could not have taken the men across the Belle Pourche to their death. Then the patrol need not have crossed the river and retreated before Crazy Bear's men, giving his medicine the boost it needed. Taken any way Dusty looked at it this whole things was his affair and it lay on his shoulders to try and put matters right.

"Ask Eagle Catcher what he wants, Sucataw," Dusty said.

"Allows somebody done took four gals of his people," replied the scout, after a shouted conversation with Eagle Catcher.

"Tell him the gals went back and the men who took them are dead."

This was relayed via Sucataw but Crazy Bear jumped his horse from the line, shook his rifle over his head and roared out angry words. Sucataw listened and spat into the dirt at his feet.

"Says we're liars, Cap'n. Allows his medicine says they can wipe us out."

That was what Dusty wanted. The reason he'd started the conversation in the first place. He wanted mention of Crazy Bear's medicine so that he could put his idea into play. He hitched up his matched gunbelt and spoke quietly, yet every man around heard what he said.

"Tell them Crazy Bear's medicine is bad. Tell Eagle Catcher to send twelve braves against me and I'll prove to him the medicine is bad."

For a moment Sucataw did not reply. Dusty's words almost took his breath away and he realized what they meant. Mark Counter jumped forward, catching Dusty's arm and turning him.

"You can't go through with a fool game like that, Dusty," he said.

"I've got to, Mark," Dusty replied. "Don't try and stop me or help me. Give Eagle Catcher my words, Sucataw. Mr. Gilbey, your sabre, please."

Gulping down something which seemed to be blocking his throat Sucataw told the watching Sioux what Dusty said. Talk welled up among their ranks, fingers pointed down towards the gate. Twenty yards

from the walls he halted, sinking the tip of the sabre into
the ground to leave his hands free.

Eagle Catcher turned, looking towards Crazy Bear
and snapping out a question. The young war-bonnet
chief gave a yell and turned his horse to ride out before
the others. Eleven more of his cronies followed, the
hard core leadership of the white-hating faction were
arrayed before their people to prove their leader's words
and medicine.

Dusty studied the men, only three had rifles for Crazy
Bear bribed young warriors into joining his faction with
the weapons gathered. The rest were armed with war
lances or fighting axes and each had a knife in his belt.
To kill with the lance, the axe or the knife was a greater
coup than with rifle or arrow and they wanted to make a
great coup to impress their people. With that small
soldier-coat leader dead the whole Hunkpapa nation
would stand behind Crazy Bear and listen no more to
the words of the old men.

With the fate of the Fort and peace to the Dakotas
hanging in his hands Dusty Fog faced the twelve men.
He knew he must take Crazy Bear with him and see this
through to the bitter end. His mistake brought it about
and he must try to rectify it alone. He allowed to inflict
enough damage on the attacking party before they got
him to weaken the desire for war in the hearts of the
other braves. Then he thought of something he must do.

"Mr. Gilbey!" he called, turning to face the Fort and
seeing almost all of the defenders gathering to see what
happened. "Turn your company about. If any man tries
to fire on the Indians—shoot him!"

Giving his wild war cry Crazy Bear sent his horse
leaping forward and the other braves followed, the
whole mass sweeping forward. Twelve men against one.
The remainder sat silent, watching. The hand of the
Great Spirit lay on Crazy Bear, his medicine was at
stake.

Joanna Lingley had somehow heard what was happening. She ran to Mark Counter's side just as Dusty gave the order to Gilbey.

"Stop him, Mark!" she gasped.

"It's too late, gal," Mark answered, face grim and hard. "And I reckon Frank Gilbey'd shoot the man who tried."

Dusty turned as soon as he'd given the order. His left hand crossed his body and the Colt left his right side. He did not hold it one-handed, but gripped the butt in both hands, raised his arms shoulder high, extended them while bending his head forward to take sight. Three-quarters of a second after his turn the Colt roared, but he'd fired an aimed shot.

A groan burst from the lips of the watching Sioux as Crazy Bear's horse went down, hit in the head by Dusty's first bullet. The young chief was taken completely by surprise for he'd never expected any man to be able to make a hit with a revolver at such a range. Pitching over his horse's head Crazy Bear crashed to the ground. His rifle flew from his hand to bury its muzzle into the earth. The chief lay stunned and dazed for a few seconds while his men charged on.

Even before Crazy Bear got to his feet he saw he was in for a harder time than he'd expected. He sprang for and grabbed up the rifle but saw its barrel was plugged with dirt, so he hurled it aside. Snatching the Green River knife from his belt he bounded down the slope passing the members of his lodge who had fallen.

With six shots from his left-hand Colt, each taken fast but carefully aimed, before the Sioux were halfway towards him Dusty had done well. Crazy Bear's horse and another were down. Three braves had dropped, the men with the rifles. A fourth, hit in the shoulder, wheeled his horse and rode back to the watching warriors.

Dusty holstered the left-hand Colt and drew the right in the same move. He threw the first shot and tumbled the nearest of the remaining warriors from his horse.

Dusty showed the gun skill which made his name a legend the length of the cattle trails in the next few seconds. His six shots each took effect, although one only dropped a horse and another struck a brave in the thigh, making him drop his lance without unhorsing him. Every other bullet struck true, bringing down a man either dead or so badly injured that he was out of the fight.

The brave who lost his horse to Dusty's second Colt lit down on his feet to charge forward, war lance held in both hands. Behind him the second brave also ran in, eager to help take coup. Bringing up the rear came Crazy Bear. The wounded man rode his horse by Dusty, unable to stop or control it. Getting control he turned the horse to get away from the fight but Crazy Bear yelled an order and he turned once more to the attack. It looked as if his aid might be needed.

Swiftly Dusty performed the border shift, tossing the revolver from his right hand to the left. He caught up the sabre with his right hand just in time to deflect the lance blow of a charging brave. In the same move, from the parry, Dusty flicked out the blade in a classic thrust. He saw the point go home into the body of the Sioux, heard the man scream. The lance fell from lifeless hands as the Indian went down.

With a wild yell the second brave bounded forward, war axe raised and the mounted Sioux came riding back, his pony picking up speed. Dusty swung to face the new menace, throwing the dead Indian from his sabre point. Then Dusty twisted aside avoiding the axe blow, he cut sideways across the Sioux's body, laying it open like slitting a melon.

Almost too late Dusty saw the riding Sioux hurling down on him. The brave left his saddle, knife in hand. Dusty did not have time to avoid the rush. He drove up the sabre and the brave's belly hit the point, his weight forcing him down on to it. Dusty was forced to his knees by the weight, he felt the sabre sinking deeper, then something burned his right shoulder like a red-hot iron. The brave, in his death throes, had ripped down his knife, laying a long gash along Dusty's upper arm. He knew the wound, while painful, was not serious and that he could fight on. He felt the sabre dragged from his hand by the weight of the dead Sioux and knew he could not get it from flesh.

By this time Crazy Bear was almost on Dusty. The people in the Fort gave a moan as they saw the small Texan facing the Sioux war chief without a weapon in his hands. Mark Counter and the Ysabel Kid exchanged glances. They knew Dusty was not so helpless as he appeared. Yet they did not know if even his knowledge of karate and ju-jitsu could save him from the knife-wielding Sioux. One thing they did know, if they offered to help Gilbey would carry out his orders. The young lieutenant stood behind his company, face set hard, revolver in his hands as he obeyed orders when his every instinct craved to turn and see what was happening.

Dusty knew the danger but he also saw a chance of living. The Sioux tribesman was not a skilled knife-fighter, not in the style of the Apache or the Comanche. For one thing he did not hold his knife the same way. He gripped the hilt so the blade extended below his hand, allowing only two really effective strokes, a downwards cut aimed at behind the shoulder or the side of the neck, or a cross rip at the ribs or stomach. Both were good in their own way, but only against a man who fought in the same manner.

Springing forward Crazy Bear lifted the knife and started it down for a neck slash, relying on his extra size and strength to drive the blade of the knife deep into the small Texan's body.

Letting his Colt fall from his left hand Dusty side-stepped and brought up both arms to block the down-coming arm. At the same moment he stepped in closer. He moved in so quickly that Crazy Bear had no chance to escape. The left hand clamped on the Sioux's wrist, the right arm bent around behind Crazy Bear's elbow and pushed it up until it was almost parallel to the ground. Then Dusty gripped the top of the trapped wrist with the fingers of his right hand, making the elbow lock complete. By keeping Crazy Bear bent backwards and held away from him, Dusty had the chief off balance and unable to either attack or get at the knife with his other hand.

Drawing back his right foot Dusty lashed it out against the Indian's shin, at the same moment he released his hold. Crazy Bear went down but came up fast, even though he'd lost his knife and limped badly. With a snarl of rage he sprang forward meaning to grapple with Dusty, for he was noted as a wrestler among his people. Only this time he met a man who had knowledge of fighting which went beyond mere wrestling. Dusty did not try to avoid the chief, he came in fast, landing on his left foot and bringing up the right karate kick which smashed under the man's breastbone.

In the time he'd been learning karate from his uncle's servant, Dusty learned the kicking tricks but he'd never used one of them with all his strength before. He saw the agony on Crazy Bear's face as the Indian reeled back then went down. He also thought he'd heard something snap when the foot smashed home but he could never be sure. Crazy Bear landed flat on his back, his body arched and blood gushed from his mouth. He would never rise again.

Not a sound came for at least a minute as everybody stared at the scene before them. Few could believe their eyes as they looked at the line of dead and wounded warriors which stretched from where the Sioux sat to around Dusty.

The small Texan stood swaying on his feet. His right arm was soaked with blood and his shirt sleeve torn, he noticed it for the first time as he bent to take up the revolver and thrust it into his holster. Dusty felt sick, physically and mentally sick at what he'd been forced to do. Since he was fifteen he'd seen death and known what it was to kill men, but never had he killed man after man as he'd just been forced to do.

A young warrior who had been an admirer of Crazy Bear let out a yell and jumped his horse forward, meaning to charge down and avenge his chief. Before the horse took three strides he was dead. Eagle Catcher's Henry came off his arm and crashed, the young brave slid over the flank of his horse and down. Then releasing the lever and trigger of the rifle, holding it at arm's length with the left hand Eagle Catcher rode down the slope.

"Don't anybody shoot!" Sucataw warned. "He's showing he comes in peace."

Standing with his feet braced apart Dusty watched the old chief riding down the open ground towards him. He heard the mutter of approval when Eagle Catcher shot the brave who tried to attack and knew he'd won. Crazy Bear's death proved the war medicine must be bad and the young warrior had no right to go against it. So Dusty waited to hear what the old chief wanted.

Halting his horse Eagle Catcher looked down at Dusty and spoke in English. "What of the four women, Captain?"

"I don't know what happened to them. The woman who had them last night says they escaped and went back to your people. One of my scouts killed the man who took them."

"I saw his body. It is in my heart that Crazy Bear did this thing to make war between my people and yours."

"And you sent him and the bad hat leaders to prove the medicine," Dusty went on. "Reckon you hoped enough of them would go under to draw their sting."

"I did. I do not want war with the white man. You have kept the treaty and I can talk peace to the braves after what they've seen."

Saying that the old chief turned and yelled an order. Men came forward to collect the bodies. They ex-

changed some startled comments as they lifted Crazy
Bear and saw the look of agony upon his face. Not one
of them offered to speak or even look at Dusty and they
turned to head back to their people. The warriors turned
their horses to ride away from the Fort.

Slowly Dusty turned on his heel. His arm throbbed
painfully and he felt very tired. He only distantly heard
the cheers of the people in the Fort and through the mist
which seemed to be swirling around him saw Mark, the
Kid, Magoon and Joanna running towards him. He
made the gates of the Fort on his feet, ignoring the girl's
gasping requests that he had his arm bandaged. There
was one thing more he must do before he could rest.

"Mr. Gilbey, take patrol and escort Eagle Catcher's
warriors to the Belle Pourche. I don't want them
meeting up with Mr. Jarrow and him trying to take
them on single-handed when there's no need to fight."

Then the world seemed to spin around and Dusty
went down in a crumpled heap at the gates of the Fort.
Mark bent and picked up his friend, carrying him
through the excited crowd toward the officers' quarters.

CHAPTER FOURTEEN

Captain Fog Resigns Command

It seemed strange to be wearing civilian clothes again after almost five weeks constantly in uniform, Dusty thought as he stood before the desk at which he'd become used to sitting and giving his orders. Now Colonel Stathern, commanding officer of the 15th Cavalry, sat at the desk and the major who would take official control of Fort Tucker stood at his side.

"You won't reconsider about the offer, Captain Fog?" asked Stathern, leaning back and looking at the small man in cowhand dress who stood before him. He might have wondered how so small and insignificant a man could take charge of United States cavalry and make them obey his will, but he'd seen Dusty in uniform and could tell a born leader when he saw one. "Stay in the army as captain, with brevet rank of major. I'll need a new battalion commander in a few months, and it's your post for the asking."

"No, thank you, sir," Dusty replied. "I'm a cowhand and I reckon that's enough for me. I rode in command of a company in the war but then I rode with them. If I took your offer I'd be tied to a desk like I've been here. It's not the same."

Colonel Strathern had arrived at Fort Tucker the previous afternoon, bringing a new commanding officer and his escort. For the first time the officers of the Fort discovered they'd been taking orders from an impostor for the past few weeks and all three could hardly believe their ears when told. Not one of them could have even started to believe Dusty did not hold an official rank.

From the moment of his arrival Stratern was aware of the high morale of the battalion. They moved and dressed like crack troops, men with pride of achievement to boost them high in their own esteem. He had been disturbed when he heard the news of van Druten's death from Jim Halter, more than disturbed when he heard a civilian, even one with so brilliant a Civil War record as cavalry commander, intended to take over a Fort and hold it together. He refused to allow Halter's return to Fort Tucker with any message until he had sent a telegraph message to General Phil Sheridan asking for advice. Sheridan's reply came quickly enough. Go immediately to Fort Tucker, look into the state of it. If he felt that Captain had maintained the Fort in anything like good order offer him a commission and brevet rank to try and persuade him to stay in the army. Next year the big push against the Sioux would commence and first-class fighting men such as Dusty Fog might make all the difference between victory and defeat.

The colonel did not need to wait until morning to make his decision. He saw enough from the start to let him know he could make the offer to Dusty with a clear conscience. He knew it still more when he read the reports, talked with the three officers, the sergeant-major and sergeants, then Joanna Lingley. From the praise all gave Dusty and the way they spoke of the small Texan, Stathern knew he could make the offer and would be pleased to have Dusty in his regiment.

Only Dusty did not accept the offer. He had done his duty as he saw it, held the Fort together and kept the peace until a new commanding officer arrived. Now he could ride back to the Rio Hondo country of Texas where his uncle would be waiting to blister his hide for wasting time. Dusty also insisted he and his friends left the following morning as they'd wasted more than enough time since selling their cattle.

Now the Colonel only talked of the subject to hold Dusty for a few moments longer while the battalion prepared a surprise for him. From the desk drawer Stathern took out a cash box which he opened.

"You held rank as captain for four, no five weeks, that's a month and a quarter's pay, two hundred dollars, plus five week's command pay at ten dollars a week," he said. "I've been authorized to pay you this by General Sheridan so I don't want any arguments. Your two pards have been accepted as army scouts for the same period of time and have been paid accordingly."

"You'll do what I asked about Sergeant Kallan, sir?" Dusty asked as he took up the money and signed a receipt for it.

"I'll mark him killed in action and put that his wife was killed in the Indian attack on Shacktown. I don't suppose you can shed any more light on how Lewis came to die?"

"I've the Kid's word that he didn't kill Lewis, sir. The Sioux got him, we found his body. I shared the money and a percentage of the gold dust we took from his safe among the people who left everything at Shacktown, then sent them east. Like I said, I sent a burial detail under flag of truce, which Eagle Catcher honored to bury the party who crossed the Belle Pourche. You'll have no more trouble around this neck of the woods for a spell."

He turned to go but Stathern asked, "Is your shoulder all right?"

Dusty nodded. "Healing. It was more messy and painful than dangerous. I can use the arm and that's all that matters. Well, I'll be going, sir. We've got a lot of miles to ride afore we hit the OD Connected and I want to cover some of them today."

Stathern came to his feet holding out his hand to Dusty. "It's been good knowing you, Captain Fog. If you're ever thinking of changing your mind and joining the army again I'll always be more than willing to have you in my regiment.''

"I'll bear that in mind, sir," Dusty replied, shaking hands.

All the time they'd been talking Dusty was aware of noise outside, the sound of men falling in for morning muster. It came almost as a shock to remember they no longer were under his command and he would not be stepping out to inspect them.

The two officers escorted him to the door and the major opened it. Outside, on the porch, rigid at a brace and with hands held in the salute stood Gilbey, Magoon and Hogan. Yet they wore their best uniforms and carried sabres as well as their pistols, dressed for a review parade.

"Battalion ready for your inspection, sir," Gilbey said.

Dusty felt embarrassed at getting in the way of the new post commander for whom the parade had been arranged. He was about to step aside but could not get by the colonel or the major who stood behind him.

"Well, Captain Fog," Stathern said. "Your battalion's waiting, sir. Take a final review."